# THE GREAT ART CAPER

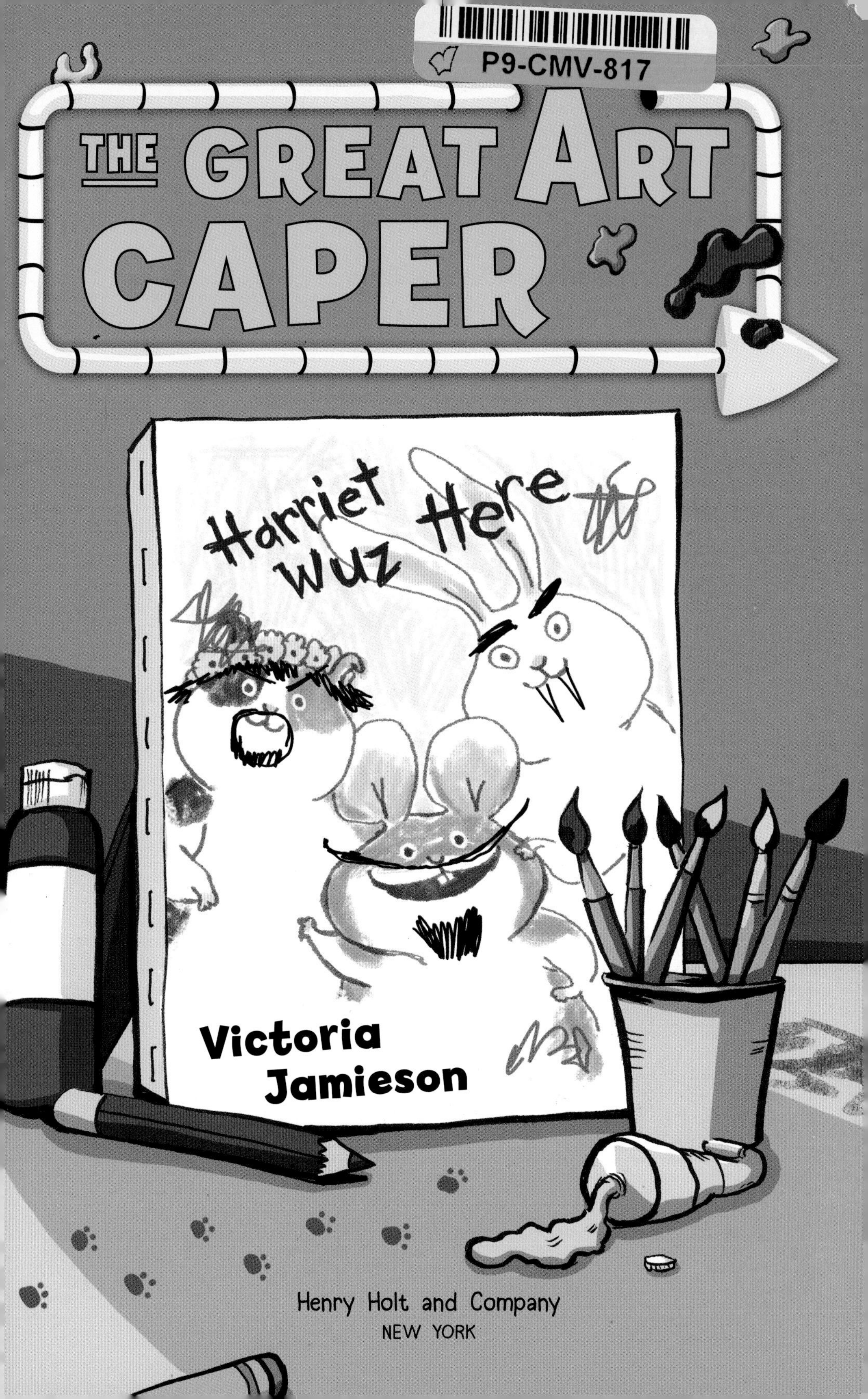
Harriet wuz Here

Victoria Jamieson

Henry Holt and Company
NEW YORK

# Chapter 1

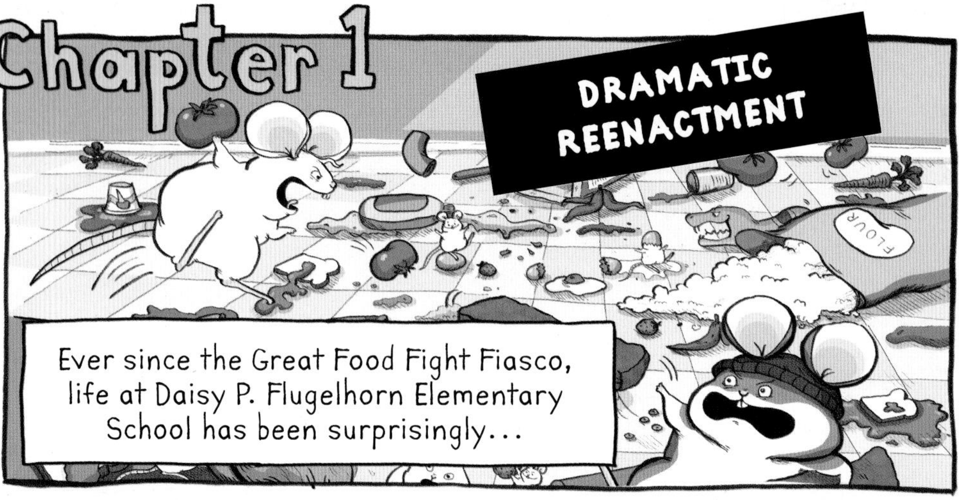
DRAMATIC REENACTMENT
FLOUR
Ever since the Great Food Fight Fiasco, life at Daisy P. Flugelhorn Elementary School has been surprisingly...

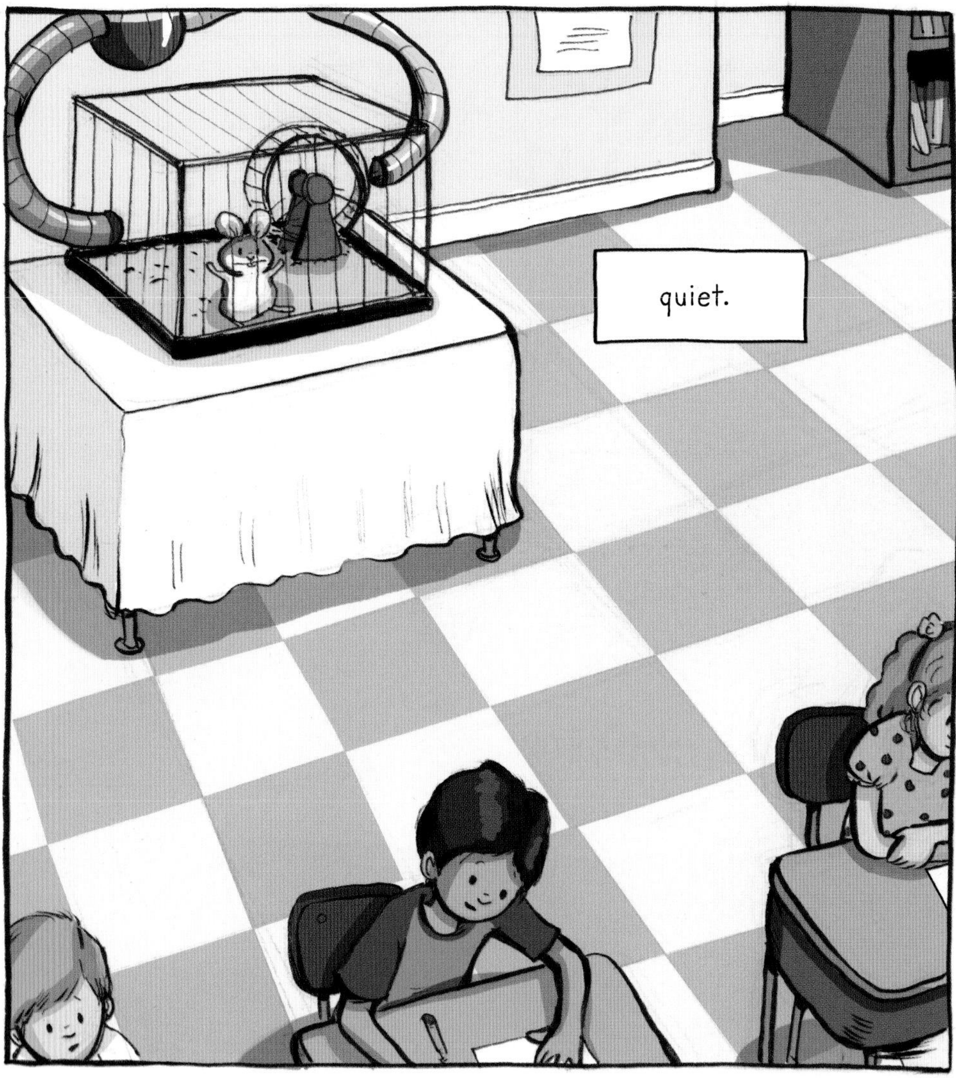
quiet.

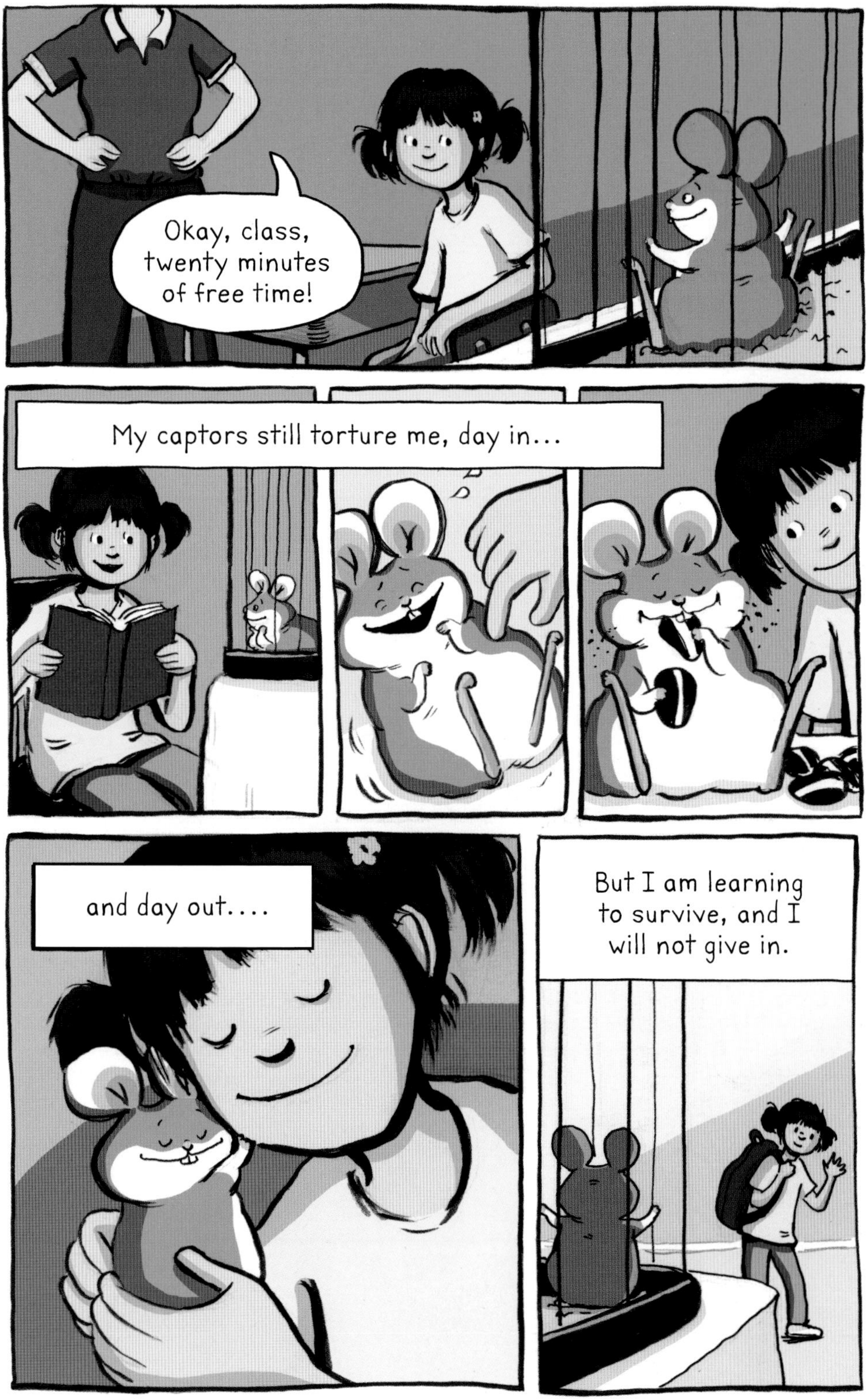
Okay, class, twenty minutes of free time!
My captors still torture me, day in...
and day out....
But I am learning to survive, and I will not give in.

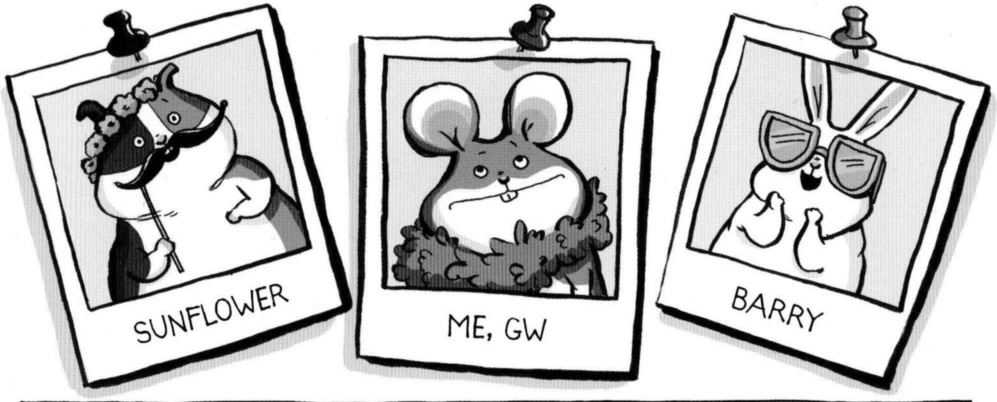
SUNFLOWER
ME, GW
BARRY

The Furry Fiends still meet up in the kindergarten classroom almost every night, but without any great battles to fight, our meetings have become somewhat tame.

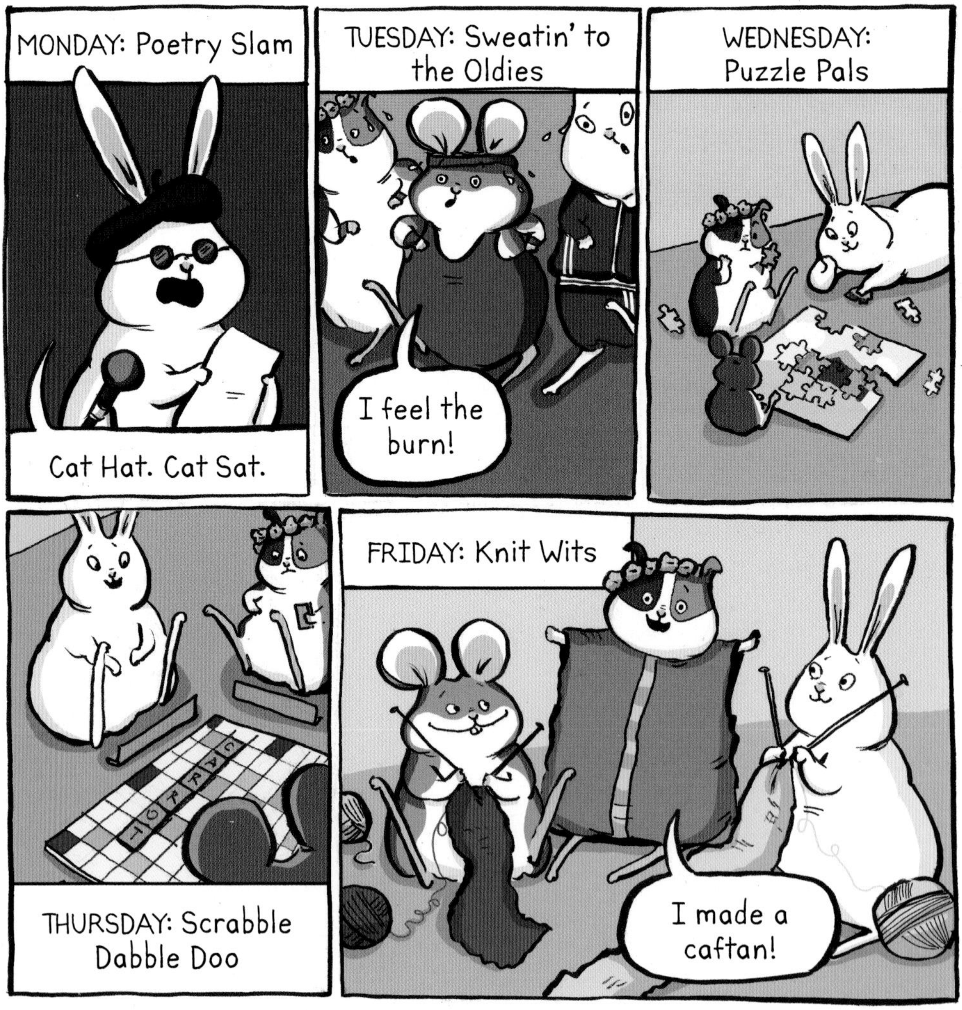
MONDAY: Poetry Slam
Cat Hat. Cat Sat.
TUESDAY: Sweatin' to the Oldies
I feel the burn!
WEDNESDAY: Puzzle Pals
THURSDAY: Scrabble Dabble Doo
FRIDAY: Knit Wits
I made a caftan!

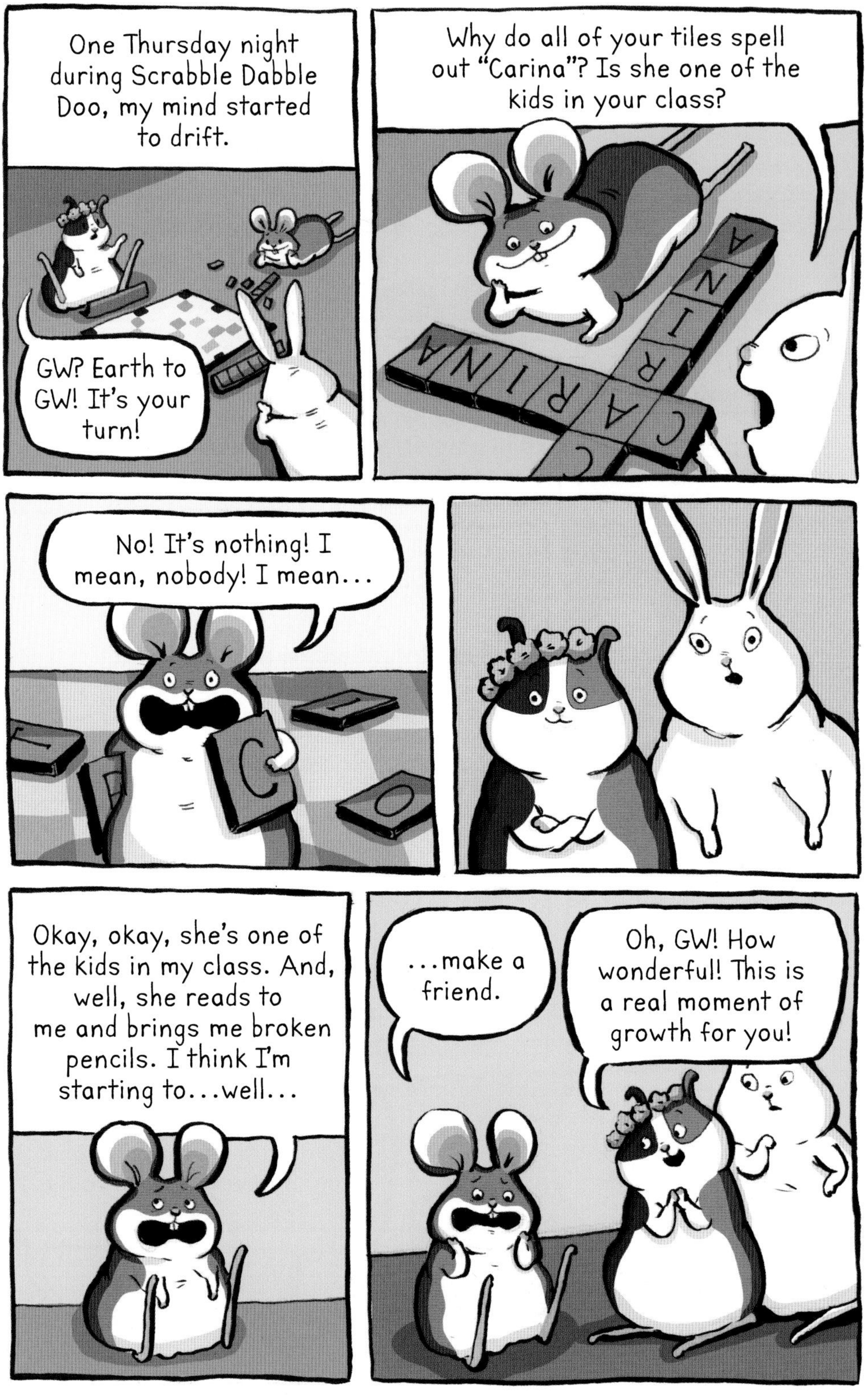
One Thursday night during Scrabble Dabble Doo, my mind started to drift.
GW? Earth to GW! It's your turn!
Why do all of your tiles spell out "Carina"? Is she one of the kids in your class?
No! It's nothing! I mean, nobody! I mean...
Okay, okay, she's one of the kids in my class. And, well, she reads to me and brings me broken pencils. I think I'm starting to...well...
...make a friend.
Oh, GW! How wonderful! This is a real moment of growth for you!

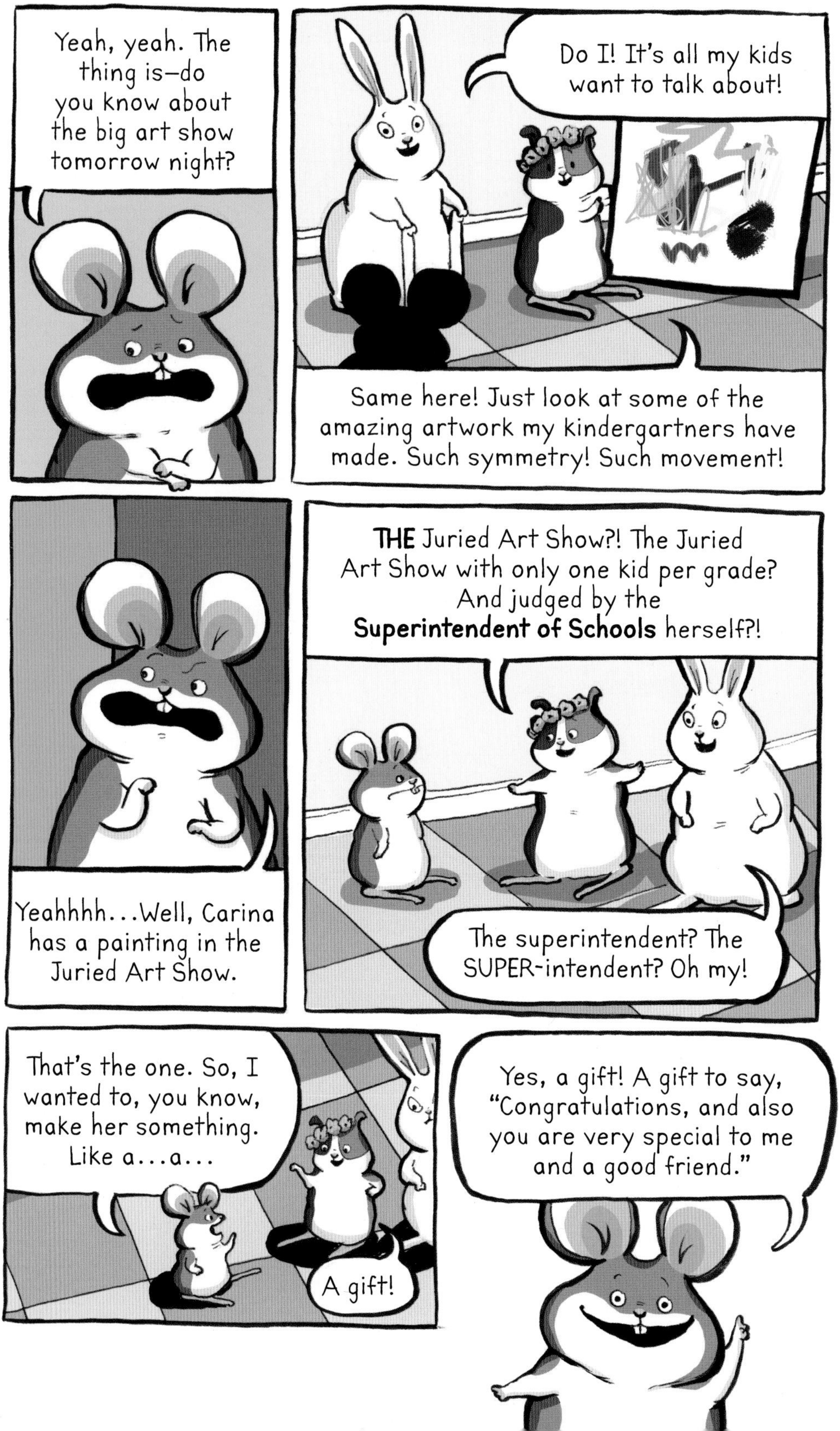
Yeah, yeah. The thing is—do you know about the big art show tomorrow night?
Do I! It's all my kids want to talk about!
Same here! Just look at some of the amazing artwork my kindergartners have made. Such symmetry! Such movement!
Yeahhhh...Well, Carina has a painting in the Juried Art Show.
THE Juried Art Show?! The Juried Art Show with only one kid per grade? And judged by the Superintendent of Schools herself?!
The superintendent? The SUPER-intendent? Oh my!
That's the one. So, I wanted to, you know, make her something. Like a...a...
A gift!
Yes, a gift! A gift to say, "Congratulations, and also you are very special to me and a good friend."

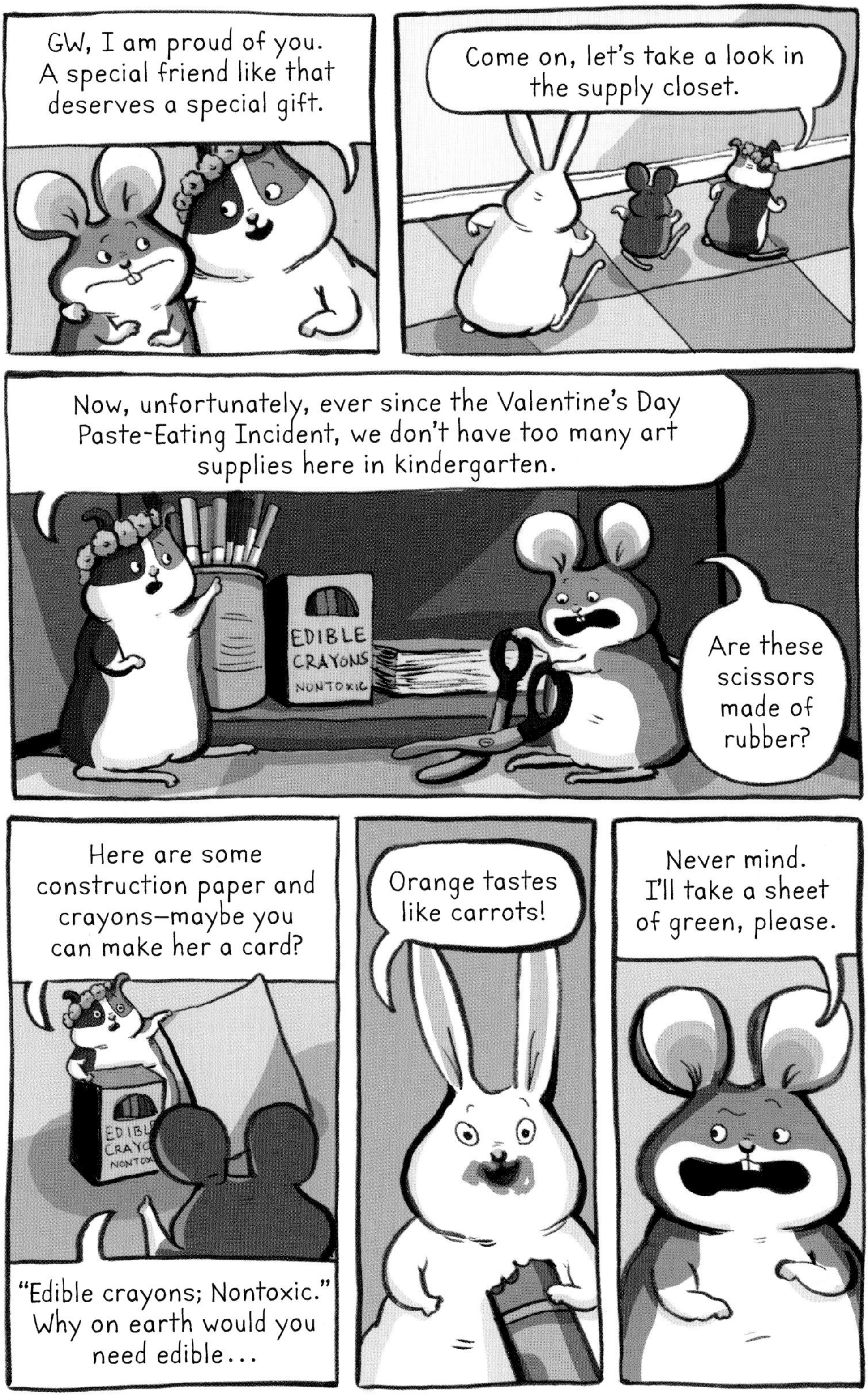
GW, I am proud of you. A special friend like that deserves a special gift.
Come on, let's take a look in the supply closet.
Now, unfortunately, ever since the Valentine's Day Paste-Eating Incident, we don't have too many art supplies here in kindergarten.
EDIBLE CRAYONS NONTOXIC
Are these scissors made of rubber?
Here are some construction paper and crayons—maybe you can make her a card?
"Edible crayons; Nontoxic." Why on earth would you need edible...
Orange tastes like carrots!
Never mind. I'll take a sheet of green, please.

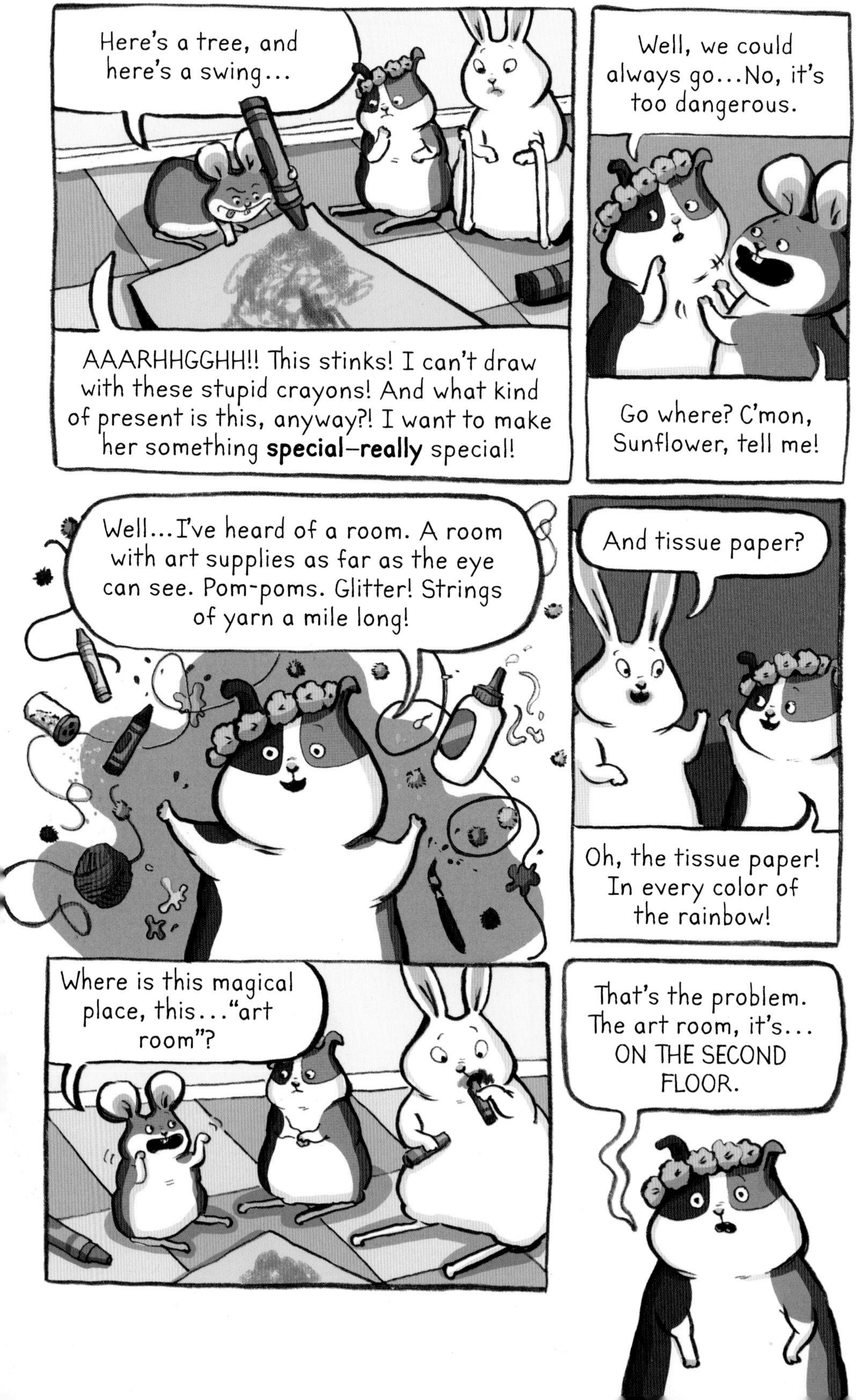
Here's a tree, and here's a swing...
AAARHHGGHH!! This stinks! I can't draw with these stupid crayons! And what kind of present is this, anyway?! I want to make her something **special**—**really** special!
Well, we could always go...No, it's too dangerous.
Go where? C'mon, Sunflower, tell me!
Well...I've heard of a room. A room with art supplies as far as the eye can see. Pom-poms. Glitter! Strings of yarn a mile long!
And tissue paper?
Oh, the tissue paper! In every color of the rainbow!
Where is this magical place, this..."art room"?
That's the problem. The art room, it's... ON THE SECOND FLOOR.

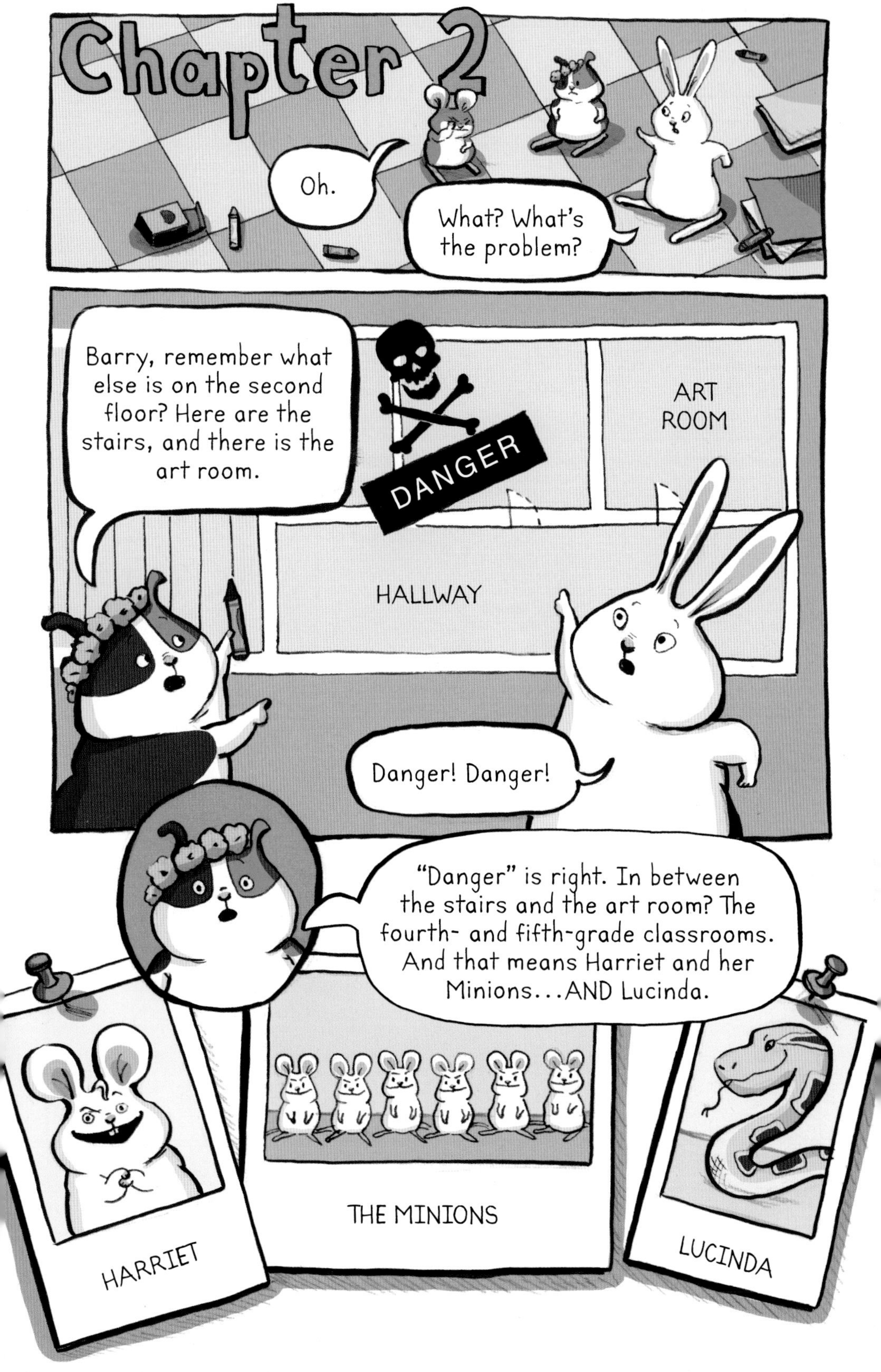
Chapter 2
Oh.
What? What's the problem?
Barry, remember what else is on the second floor? Here are the stairs, and there is the art room.
DANGER
ART ROOM
HALLWAY
Danger! Danger!
"Danger" is right. In between the stairs and the art room? The fourth- and fifth-grade classrooms. And that means Harriet and her Minions...AND Lucinda.
HARRIET
THE MINIONS
LUCINDA

Harriet's left us alone recently. Maybe she's turned nice?

Get real, Barry.

She was awfully angry after her Lunchtime Surprise scheme failed. I don't like going so close to her classroom—it's too dangerous. Forget I mentioned it.

But what about the glitter? And the pom-poms? And the...tissue paper?

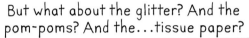

And what about my present for Carina? We've faced dangerous situations before. Isn't it worth taking a little risk to do something nice for a friend?

Okay, okay. But it won't be easy. For one thing, we have to figure out a way to get up those stairs!

Don't worry about that! Bring your helmets and meet me by the stairs in ten minutes!

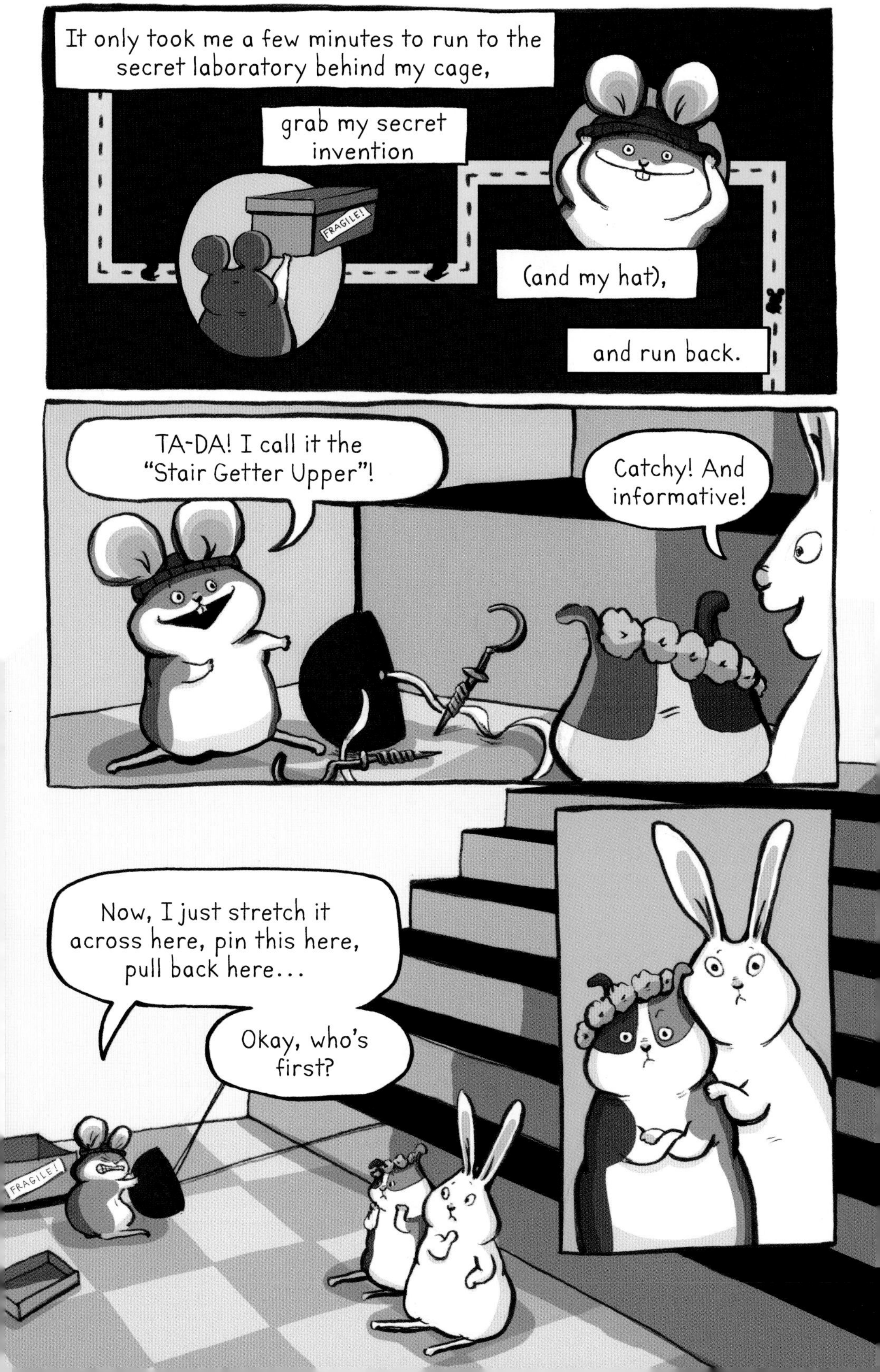
It only took me a few minutes to run to the secret laboratory behind my cage,
grab my secret invention
FRAGILE!
(and my hat),
and run back.
TA-DA! I call it the "Stair Getter Upper"!
Catchy! And informative!
Now, I just stretch it across here, pin this here, pull back here...
Okay, who's first?
FRAGILE!

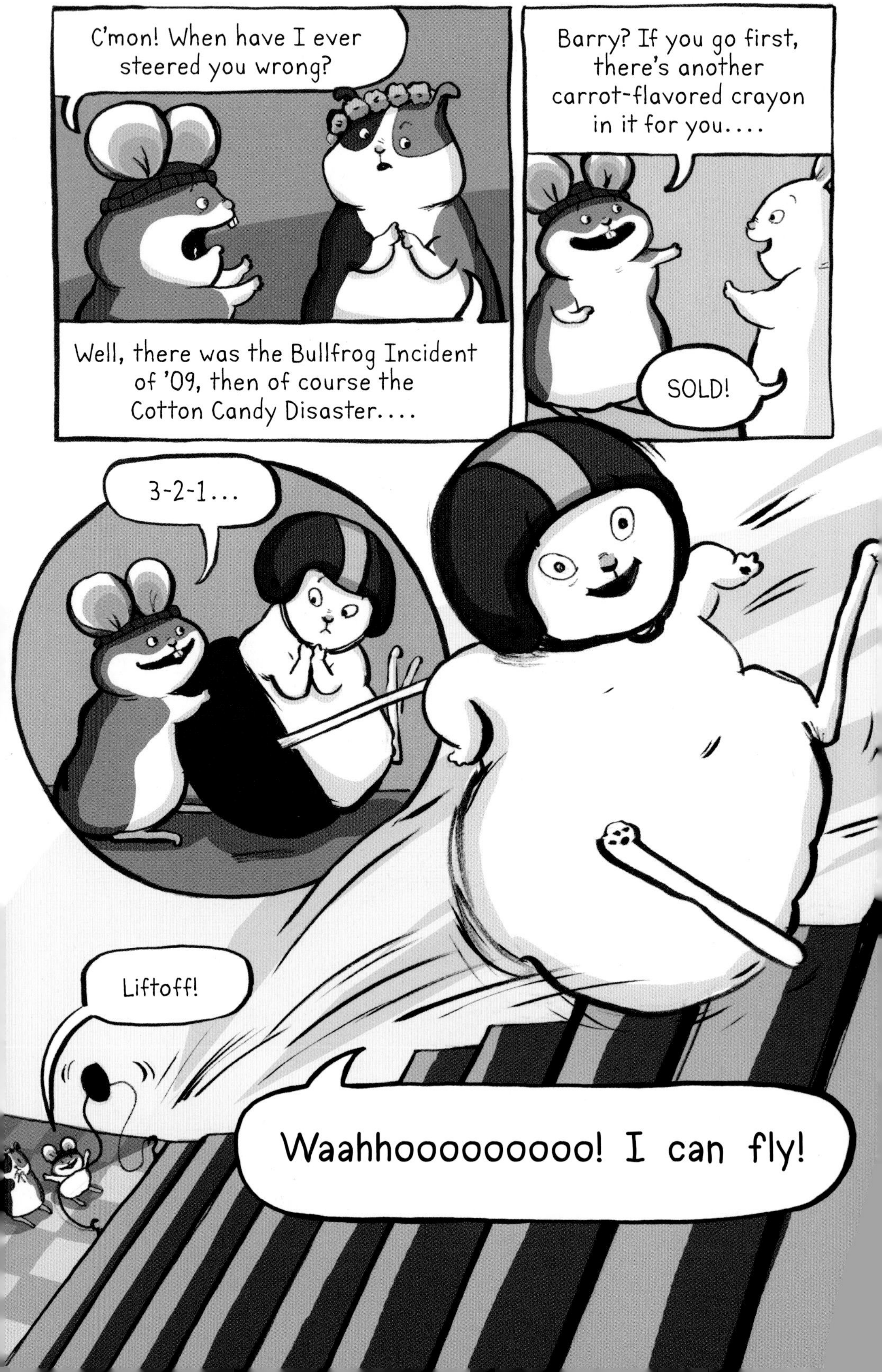
C'mon! When have I ever steered you wrong?
Well, there was the Bullfrog Incident of '09, then of course the Cotton Candy Disaster....
Barry? If you go first, there's another carrot-flavored crayon in it for you....
SOLD!
3-2-1...
Liftoff!
Waahhooooooooo! I can fly!

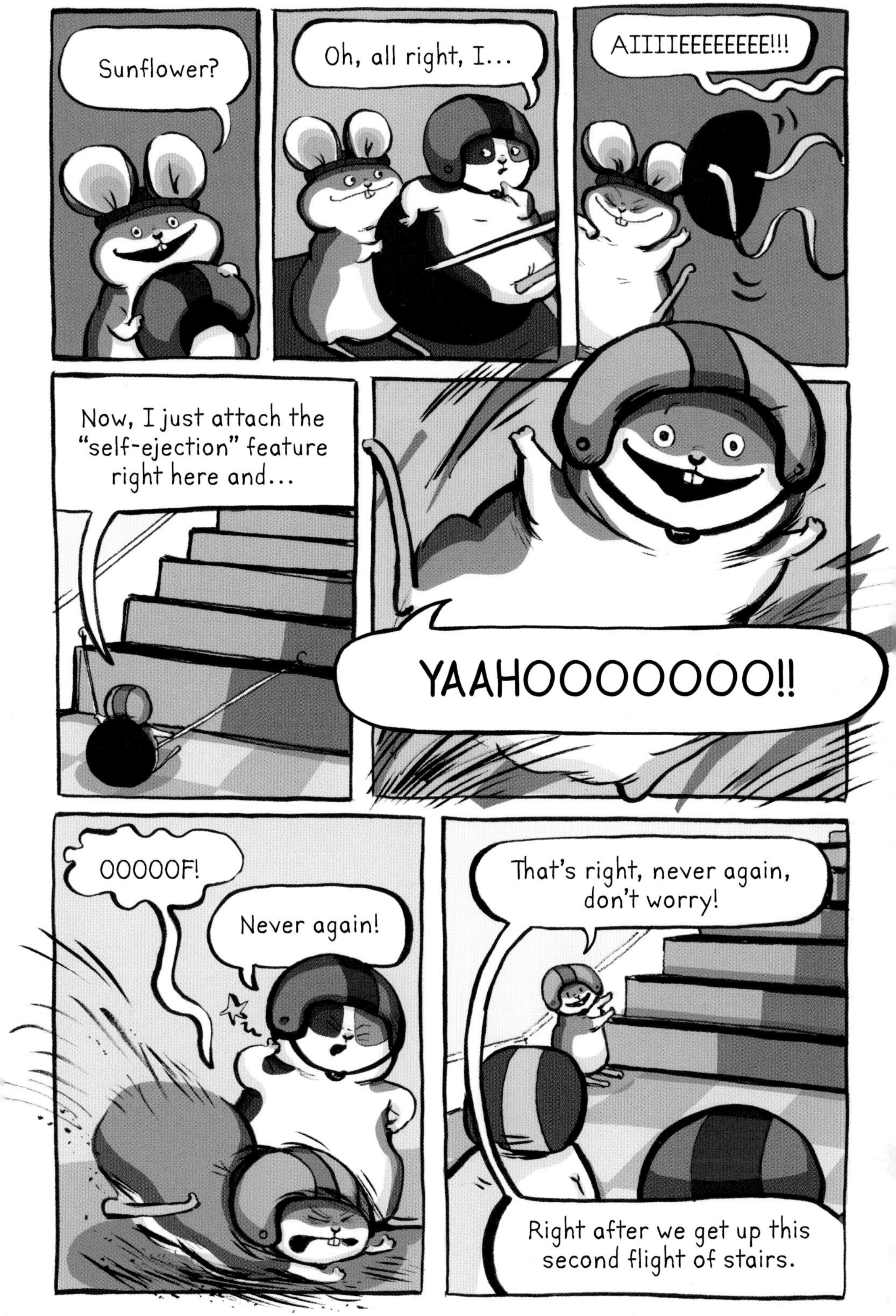
Sunflower?
Oh, all right, I...
AIIIIEEEEEEEE!!!
Now, I just attach the "self-ejection" feature right here and...
YAAHOOOOOOOO!!
OOOOOF!
Never again!
That's right, never again, don't worry!
Right after we get up this second flight of stairs.

# Chapter 3

Okay, the art room is at the end of this hallway. Those are the fourth- and fifth-grade classrooms.

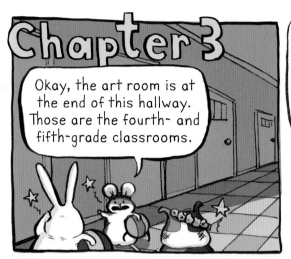

Now, to sneak past, I propose we try the classic "Bait and Switch" trick, or perhaps #415, "the Waltz." What do you think, Sunflower? Barry?

Barry! Come back!!

The coast is clear! And...Oh. Oh my. I've never seen anything so beautiful in my entire life!!

Oh boy. Come on, we'd better go get him. I can't believe he just wandered off without waiting for a plan... highly unorthodox, highly...

WHOA.

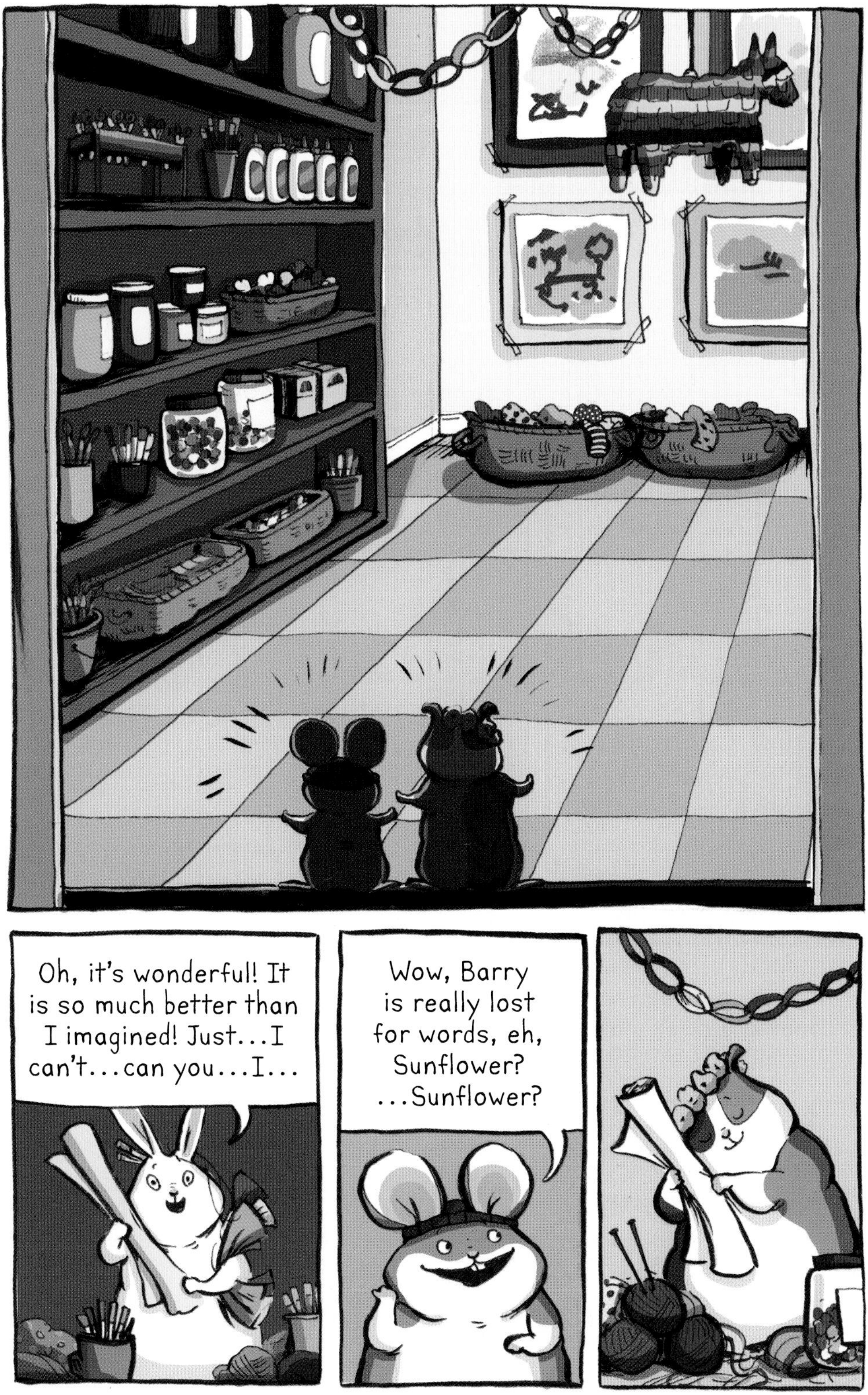
Oh, it's wonderful! It is so much better than I imagined! Just...I can't...can you...I...
Wow, Barry is really lost for words, eh, Sunflower? ...Sunflower?

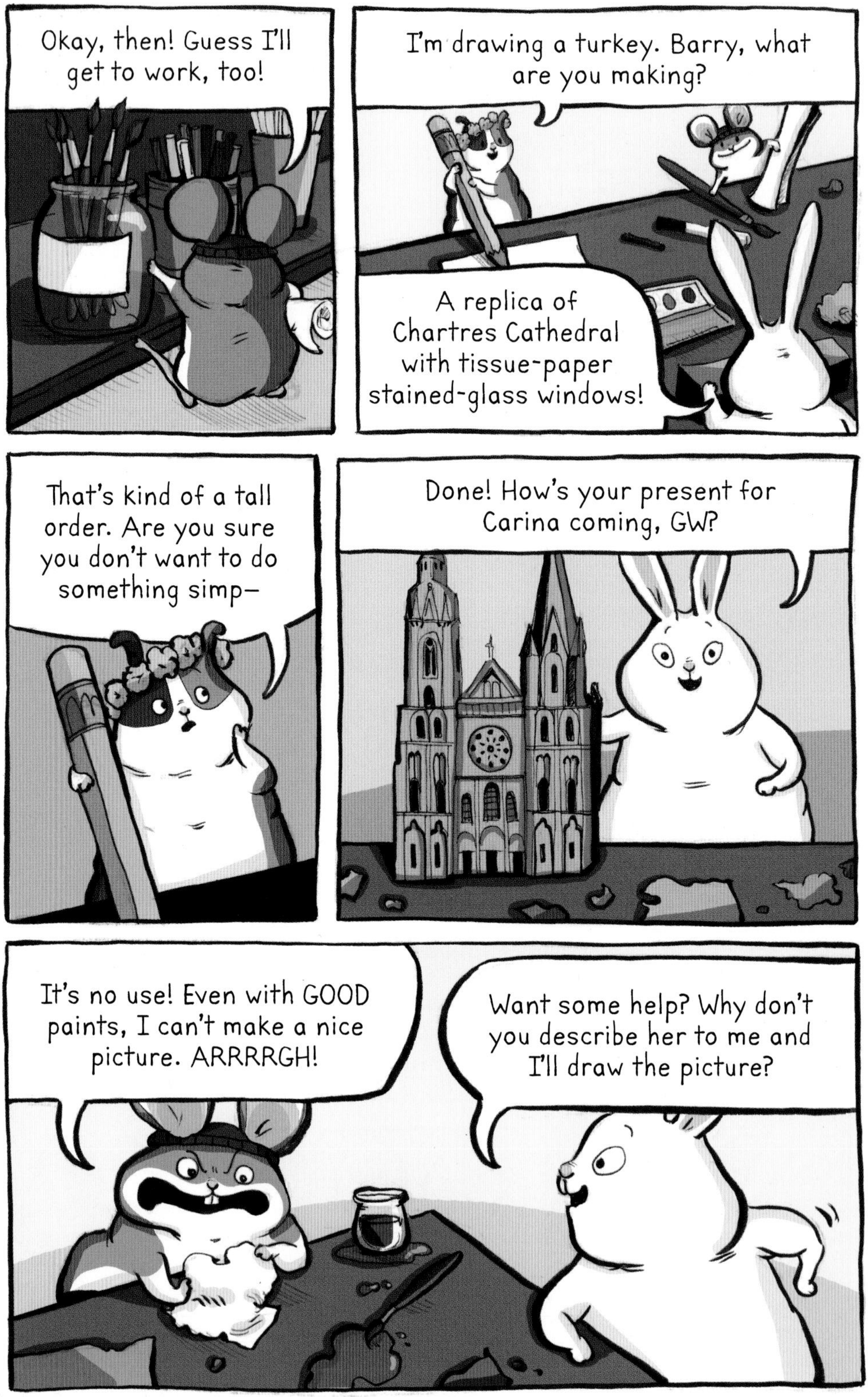
Okay, then! Guess I'll get to work, too!
I'm drawing a turkey. Barry, what are you making?
A replica of Chartres Cathedral with tissue-paper stained-glass windows!
That's kind of a tall order. Are you sure you don't want to do something simp–
Done! How's your present for Carina coming, GW?
It's no use! Even with GOOD paints, I can't make a nice picture. ARRRRGH!
Want some help? Why don't you describe her to me and I'll draw the picture?

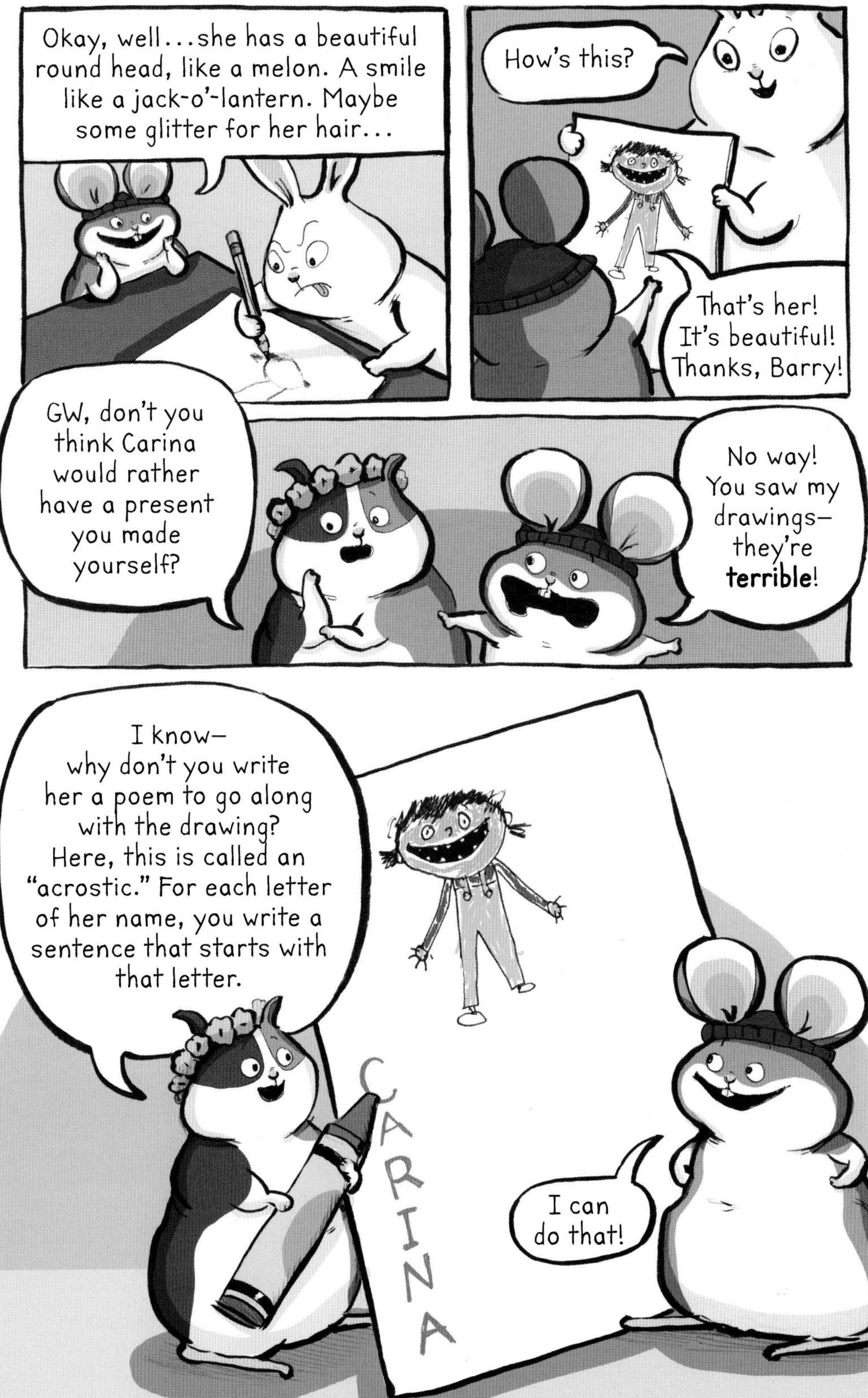
Okay, well...she has a beautiful round head, like a melon. A smile like a jack-o'-lantern. Maybe some glitter for her hair...
How's this?
That's her! It's beautiful! Thanks, Barry!
GW, don't you think Carina would rather have a present you made yourself?
No way! You saw my drawings—they're **terrible**!
I know—why don't you write her a poem to go along with the drawing? Here, this is called an "acrostic." For each letter of her name, you write a sentence that starts with that letter.
CARINA
I can do that!

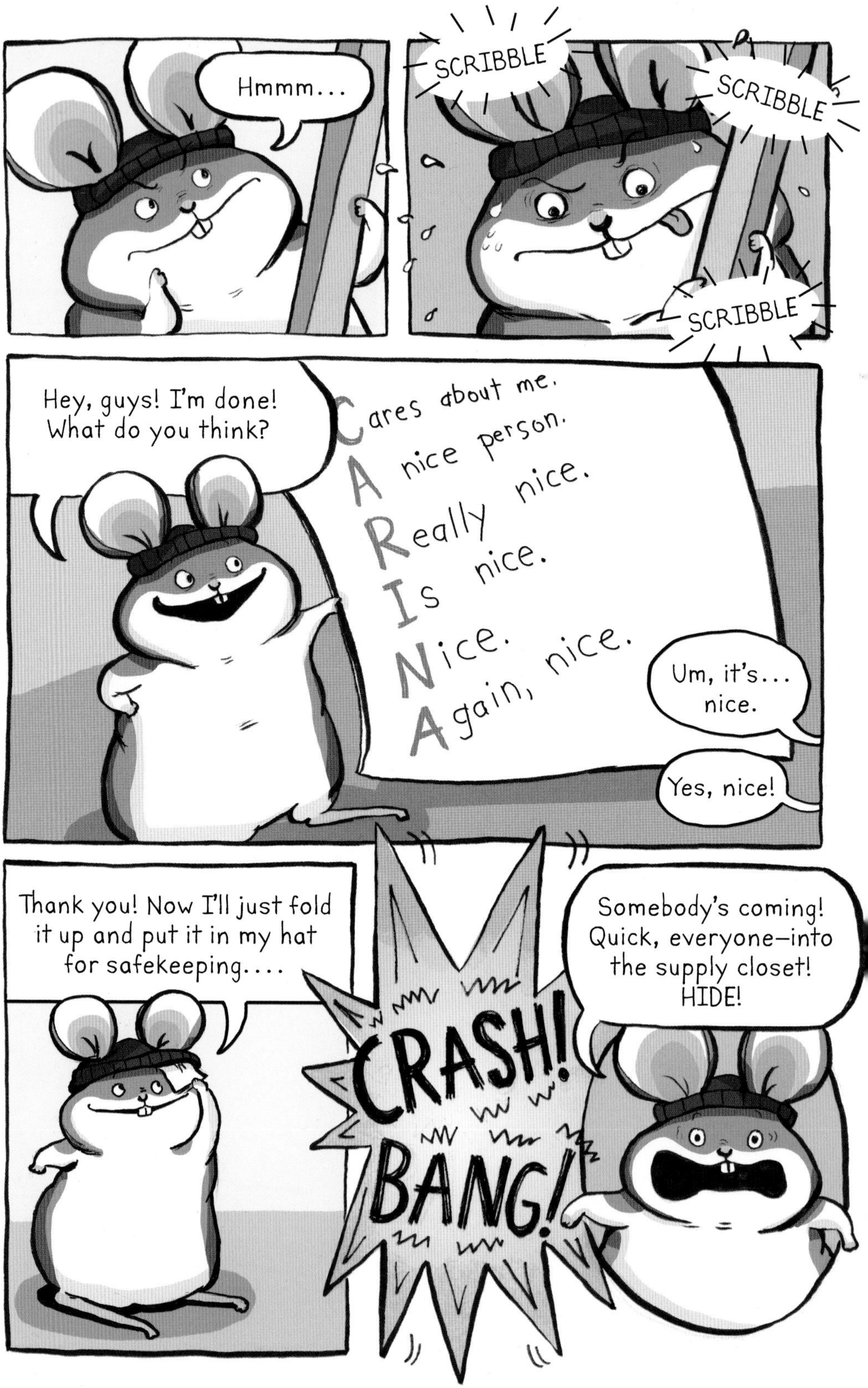
Hmmm...
SCRIBBLE
SCRIBBLE
SCRIBBLE
Hey, guys! I'm done! What do you think?
Cares about me.
A nice person.
Really nice.
Is nice.
Nice.
Again, nice.
Um, it's... nice.
Yes, nice!
Thank you! Now I'll just fold it up and put it in my hat for safekeeping....
CRASH!
BANG!
Somebody's coming! Quick, everyone—into the supply closet! HIDE!

# Chapter 4

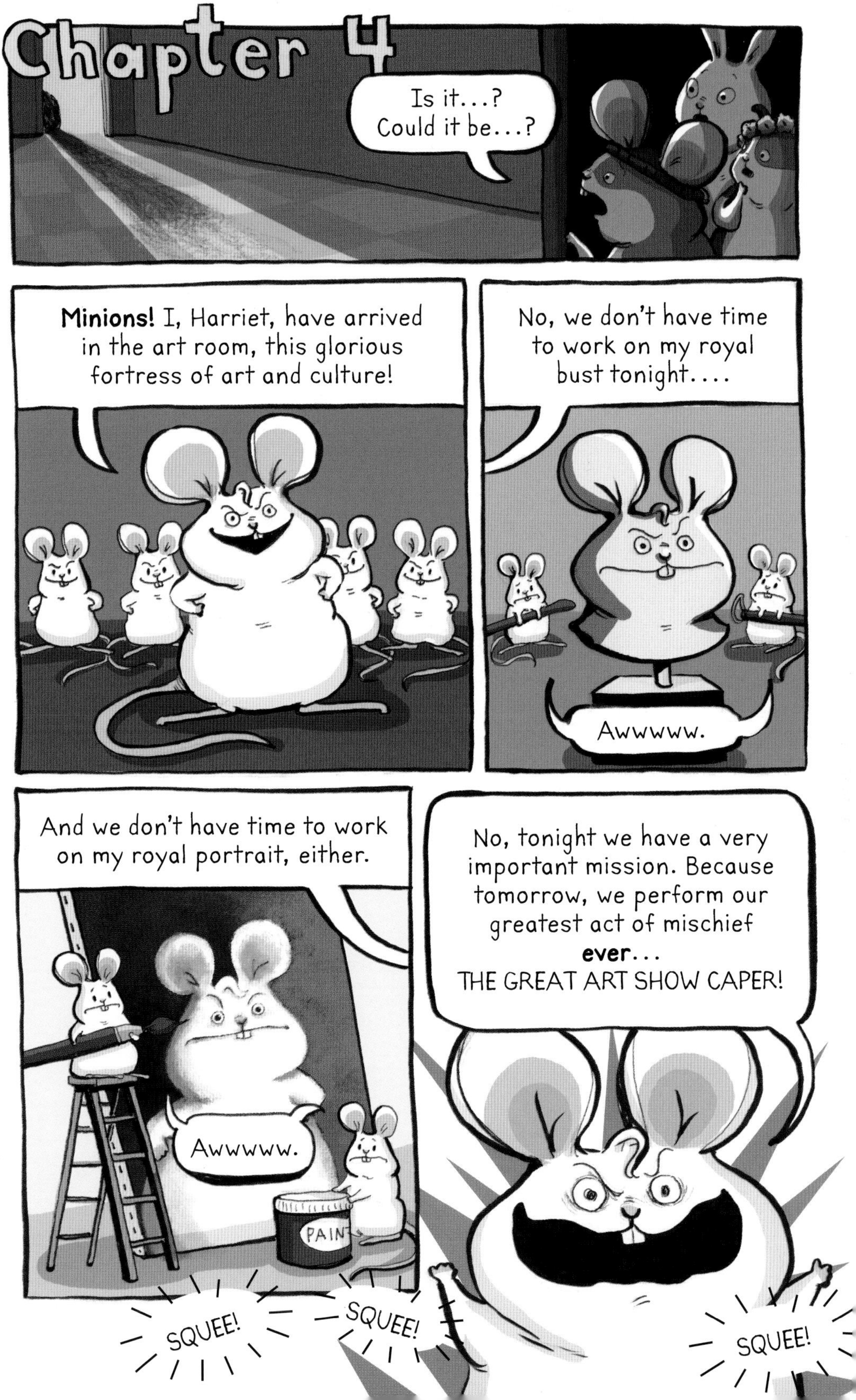

Is it...? Could it be...?
**Minions!** I, Harriet, have arrived in the art room, this glorious fortress of art and culture!
No, we don't have time to work on my royal bust tonight....
Awwwww.
And we don't have time to work on my royal portrait, either.
Awwwww.
PAINT
No, tonight we have a very important mission. Because tomorrow, we perform our greatest act of mischief **ever**... THE GREAT ART SHOW CAPER!
SQUEE!
SQUEE!
SQUEE!

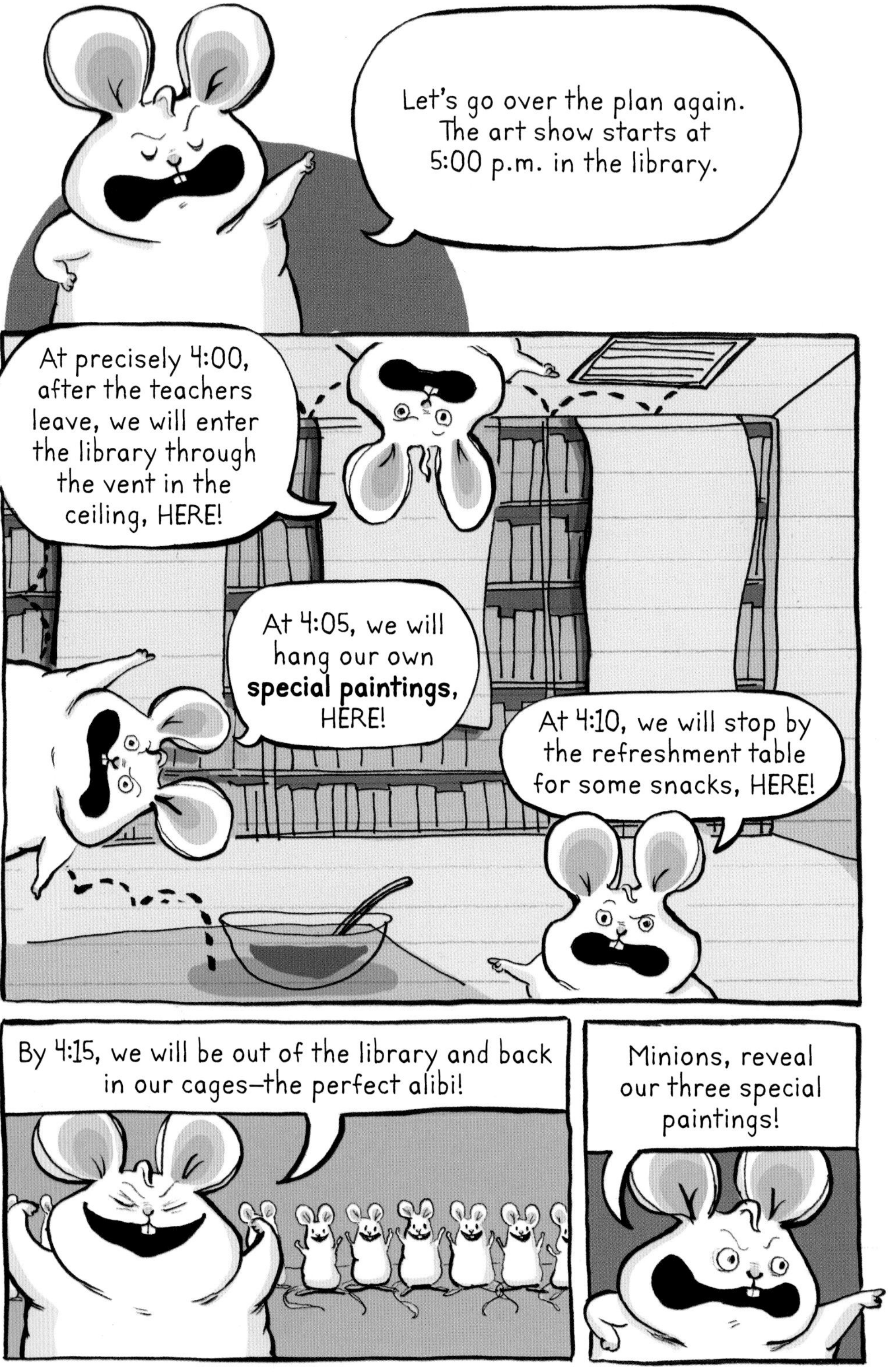
Let's go over the plan again. The art show starts at 5:00 p.m. in the library.
At precisely 4:00, after the teachers leave, we will enter the library through the vent in the ceiling, HERE!
At 4:05, we will hang our own **special paintings,** HERE!
At 4:10, we will stop by the refreshment table for some snacks, HERE!
By 4:15, we will be out of the library and back in our cages—the perfect alibi!
Minions, reveal our three special paintings!

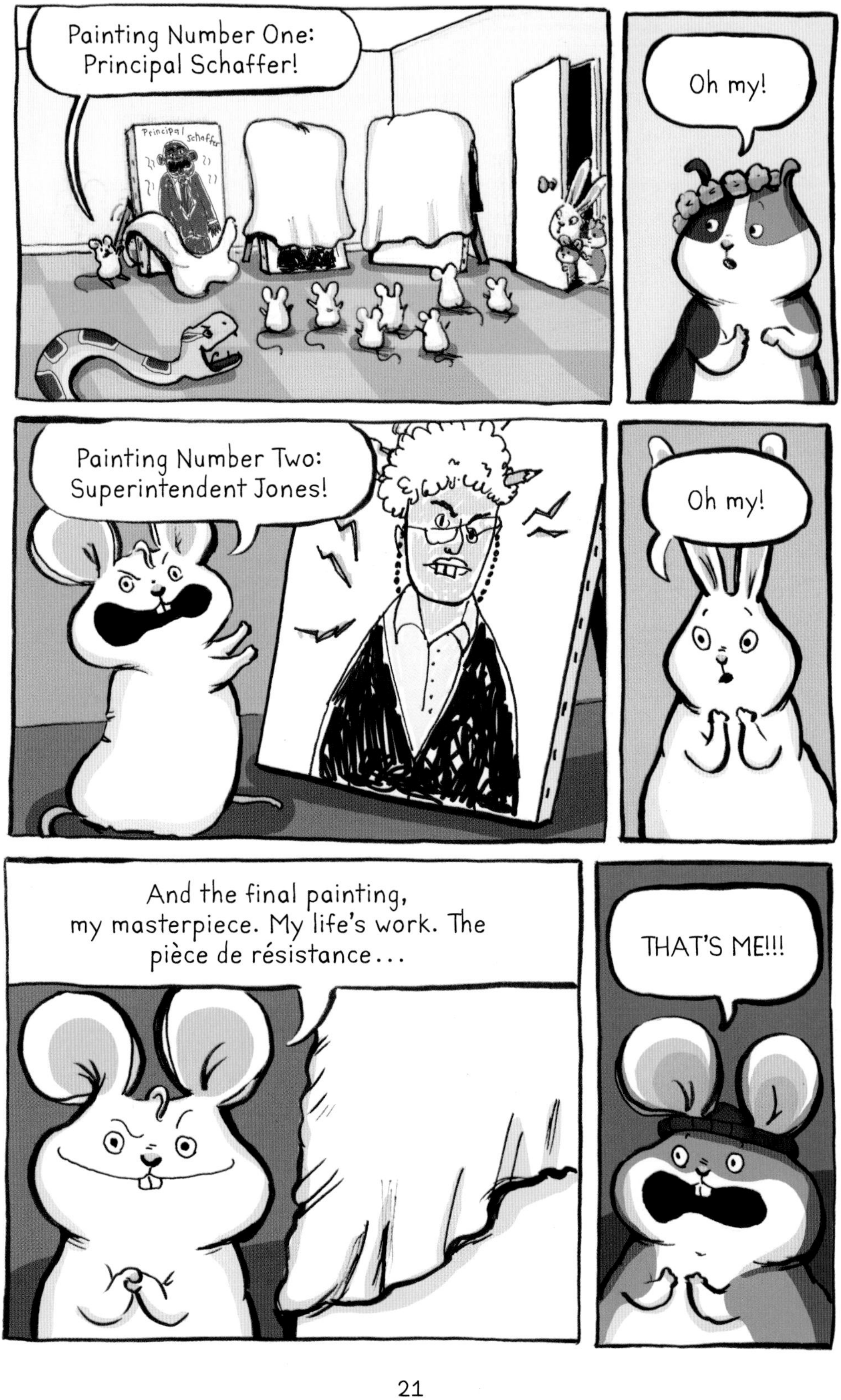
Painting Number One:
Principal Schaffer!
Principal Schaffer
Oh my!
Painting Number Two:
Superintendent Jones!
Oh my!
And the final painting,
my masterpiece. My life's work. The
pièce de résistance…
THAT'S ME!!!

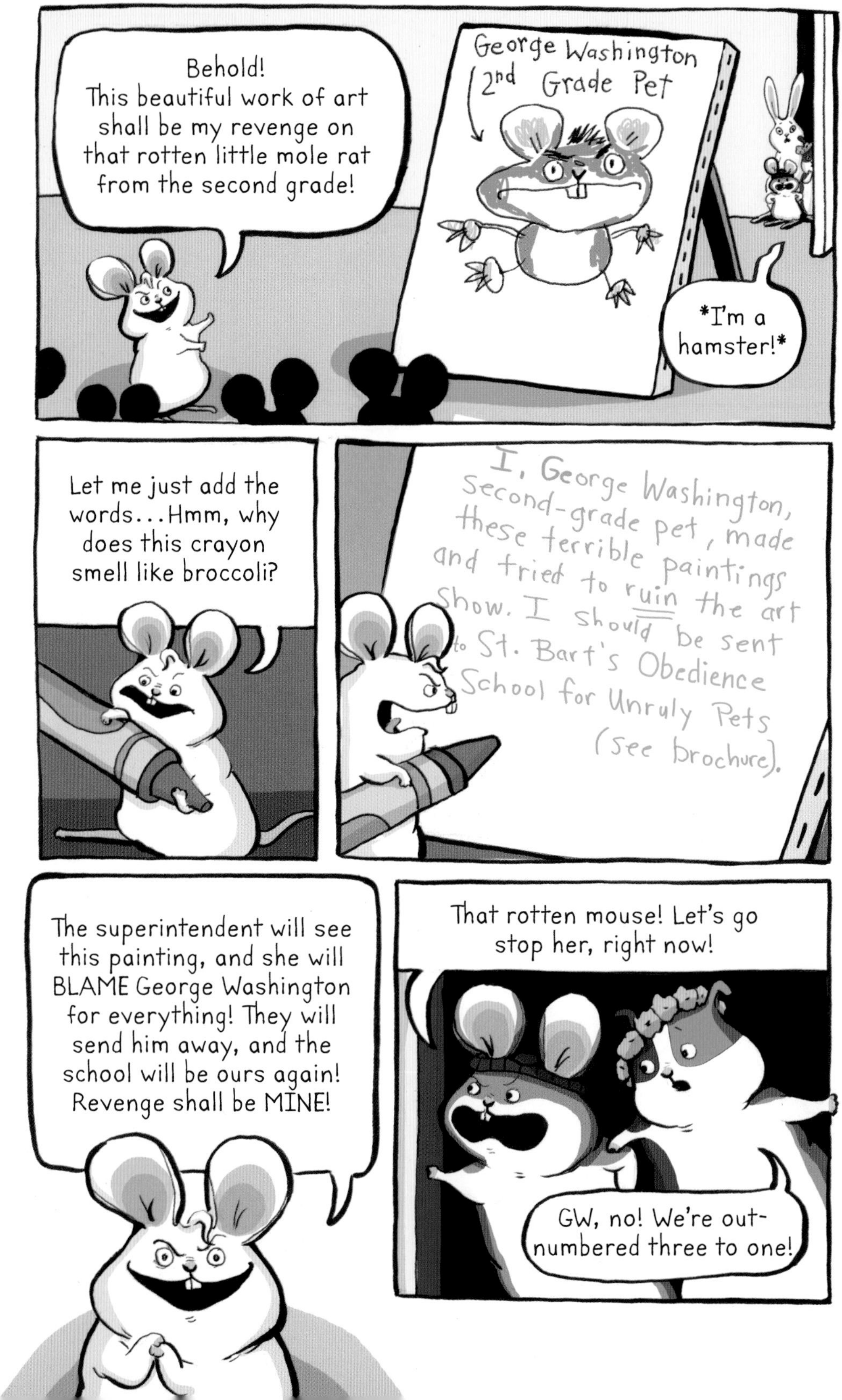
Behold! This beautiful work of art shall be my revenge on that rotten little mole rat from the second grade!
George Washington 2nd Grade Pet
*I'm a hamster!*
Let me just add the words...Hmm, why does this crayon smell like broccoli?
I, George Washington, Second-grade pet, made these terrible paintings and tried to ruin the art show. I should be sent to St. Bart's Obedience School for Unruly Pets (see brochure).
The superintendent will see this painting, and she will BLAME George Washington for everything! They will send him away, and the school will be ours again! Revenge shall be MINE!
That rotten mouse! Let's go stop her, right now!
GW, no! We're out-numbered three to one!

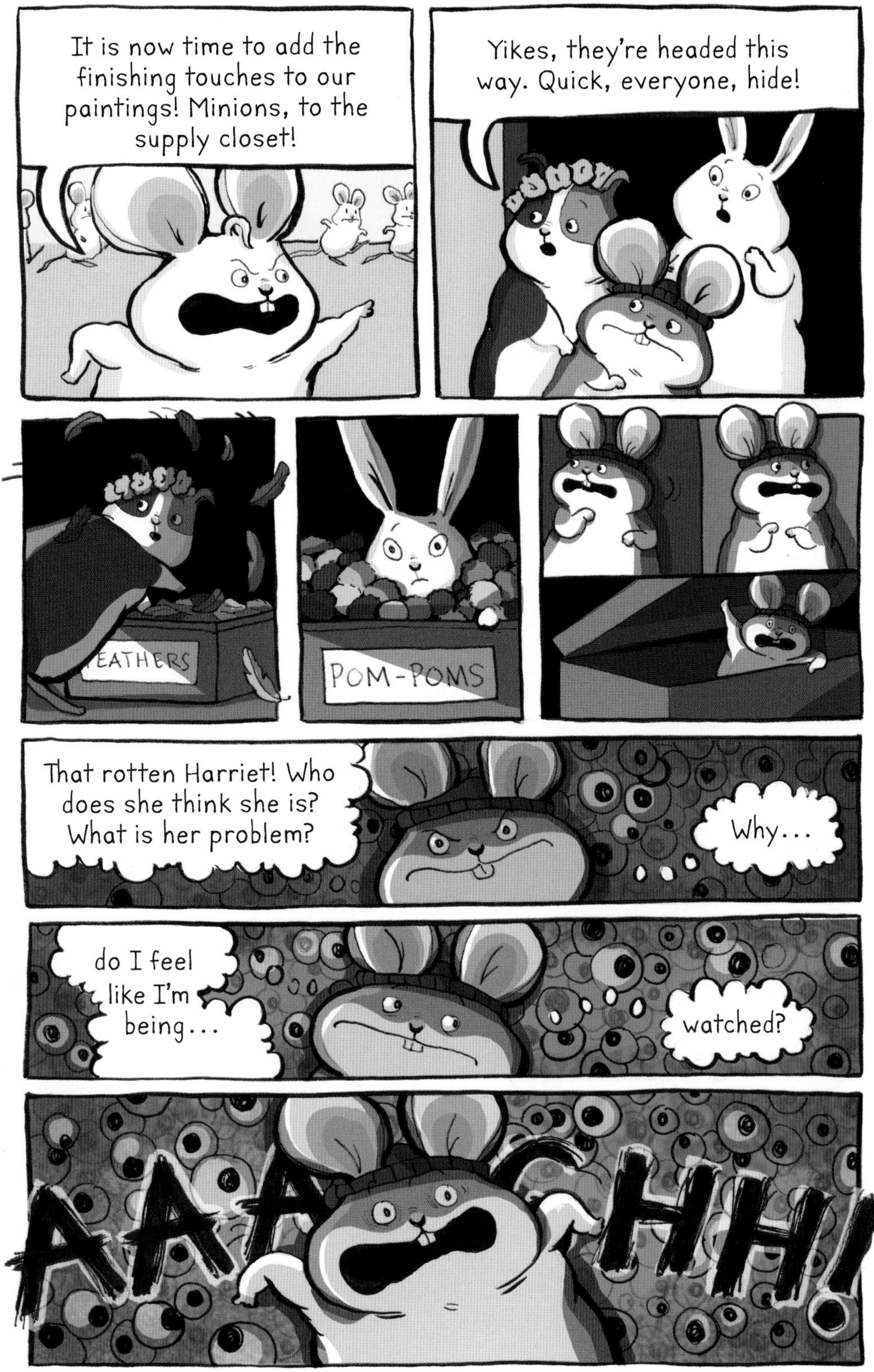
It is now time to add the finishing touches to our paintings! Minions, to the supply closet!
Yikes, they're headed this way. Quick, everyone, hide!
EATHERS
POM-POMS
That rotten Harriet! Who does she think she is? What is her problem?
Why...
do I feel like I'm being...
watched?
AAAAHHH!

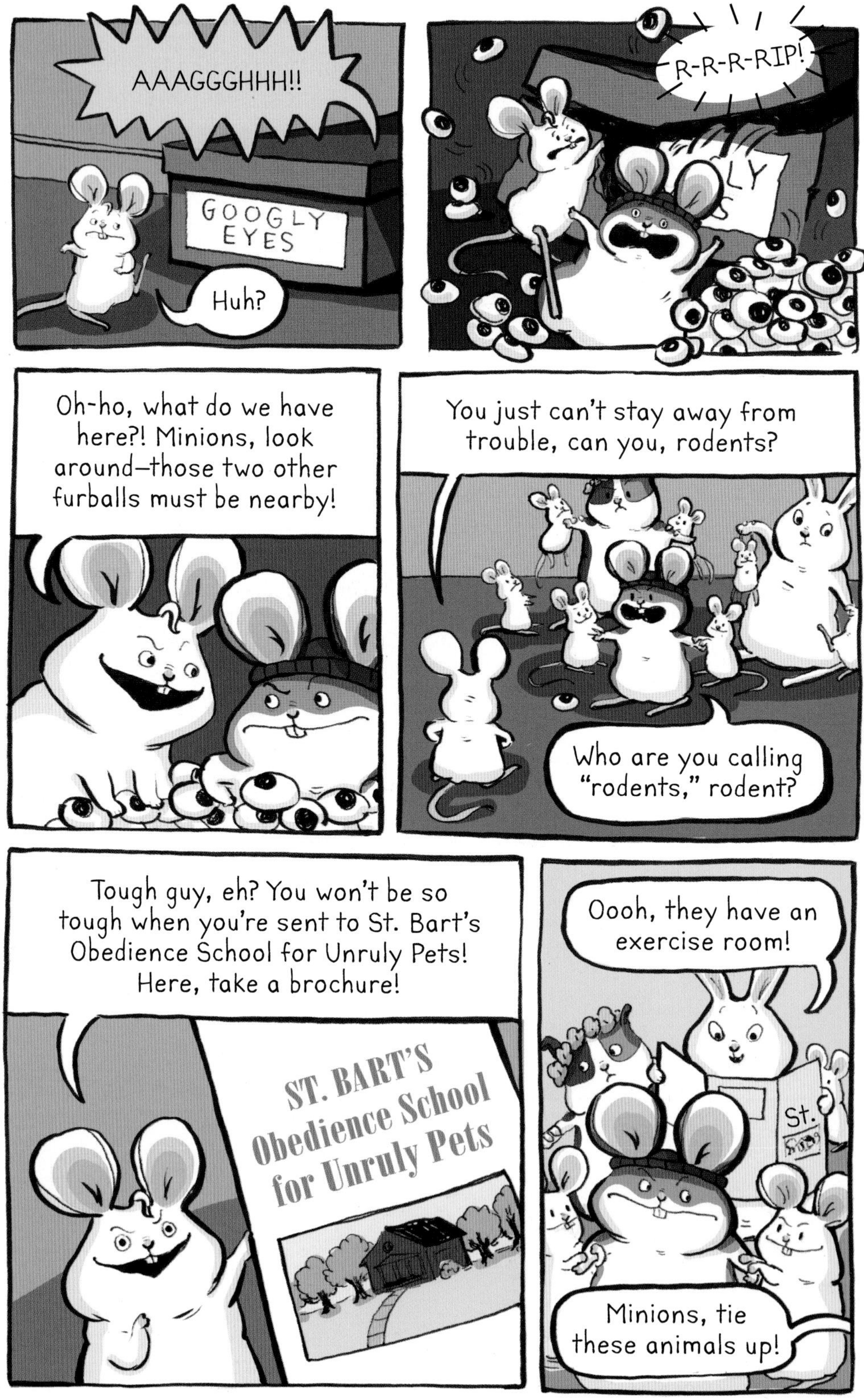
AAAGGGHHH!!
GOOGLY EYES
Huh?
R-R-R-RIP!
Oh-ho, what do we have here?! Minions, look around—those two other furballs must be nearby!
You just can't stay away from trouble, can you, rodents?
Who are you calling "rodents," rodent?
Tough guy, eh? You won't be so tough when you're sent to St. Bart's Obedience School for Unruly Pets! Here, take a brochure!
ST. BART'S Obedience School for Unruly Pets
Oooh, they have an exercise room!
St.
Minions, tie these animals up!

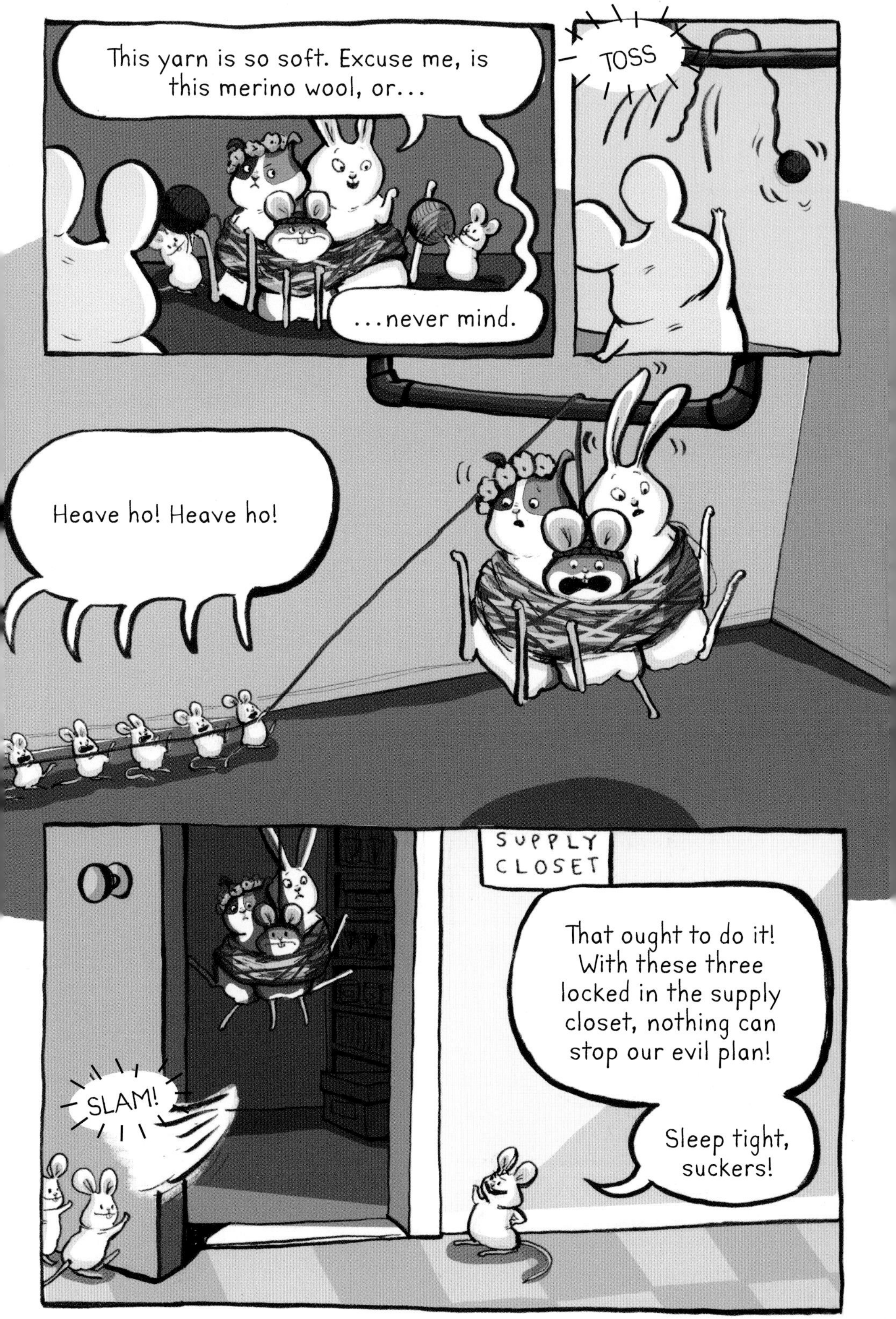
This yarn is so soft. Excuse me, is this merino wool, or...
...never mind.
TOSS
Heave ho! Heave ho!
SUPPLY CLOSET
That ought to do it! With these three locked in the supply closet, nothing can stop our evil plan!
Sleep tight, suckers!
SLAM!

# Chapter 5

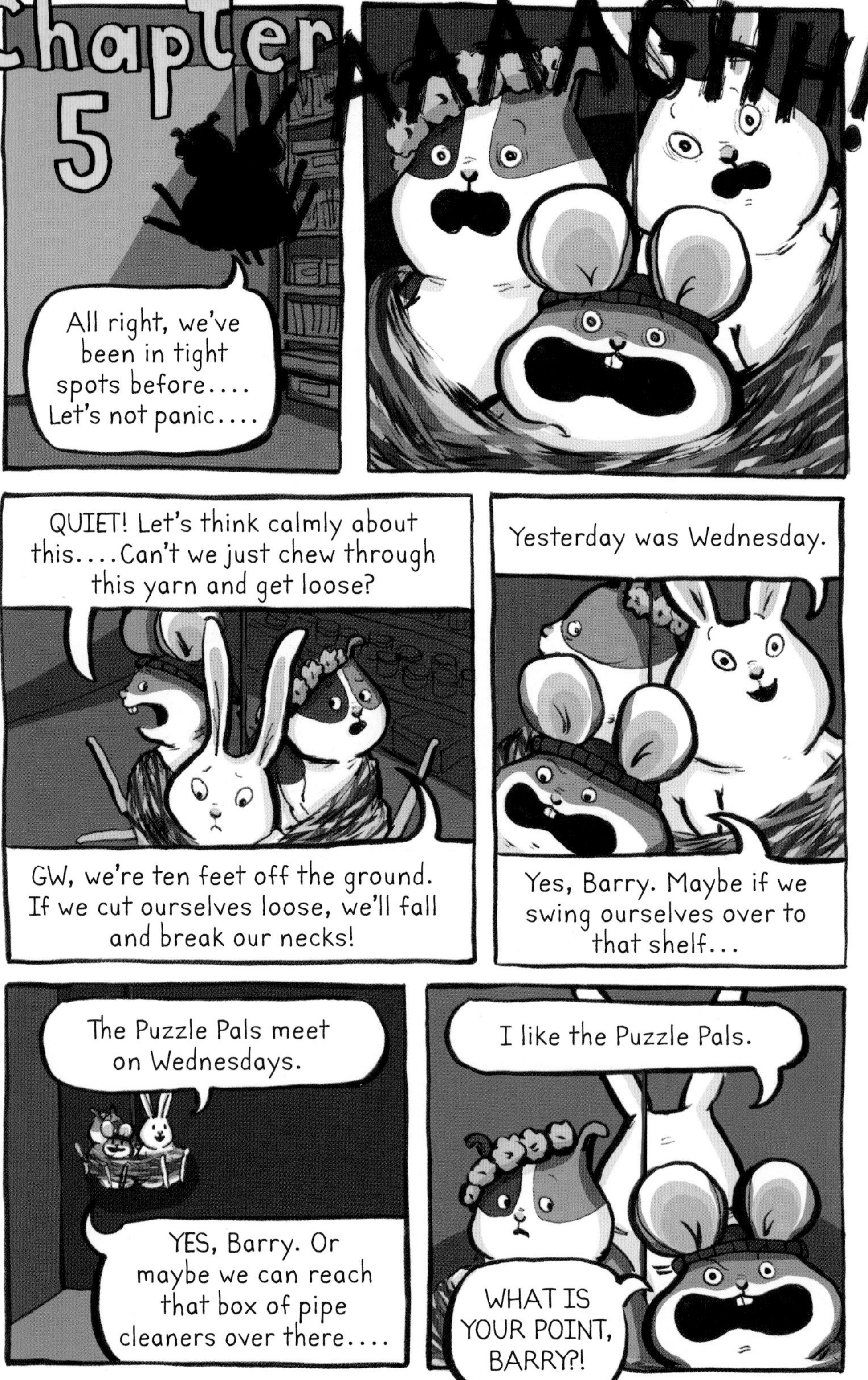
All right, we've been in tight spots before.... Let's not panic....
AAAAGHH!
QUIET! Let's think calmly about this....Can't we just chew through this yarn and get loose?
GW, we're ten feet off the ground. If we cut ourselves loose, we'll fall and break our necks!
Yesterday was Wednesday.
Yes, Barry. Maybe if we swing ourselves over to that shelf...
The Puzzle Pals meet on Wednesdays.
YES, Barry. Or maybe we can reach that box of pipe cleaners over there....
I like the Puzzle Pals.
WHAT IS YOUR POINT, BARRY?!

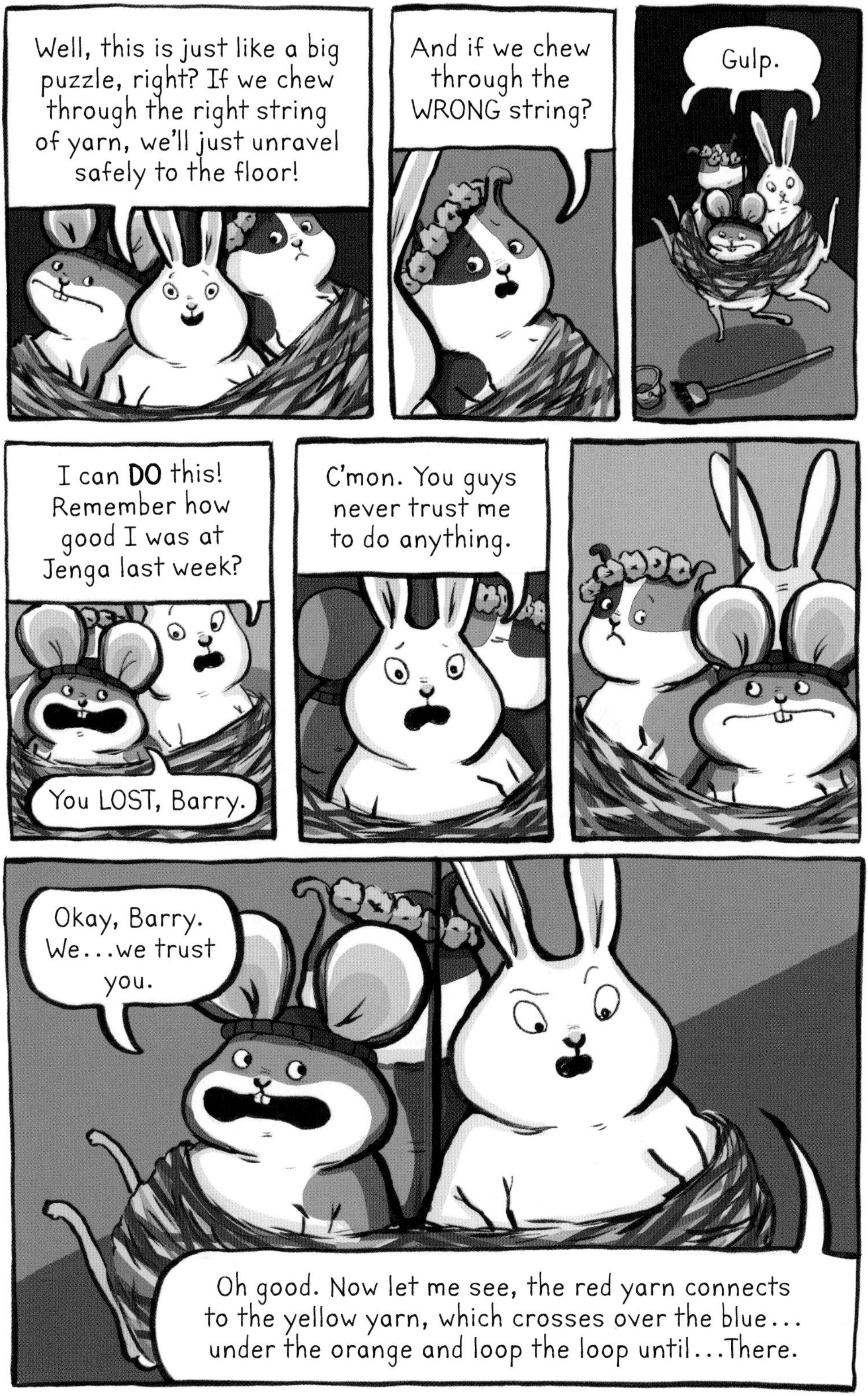
Well, this is just like a big puzzle, right? If we chew through the right string of yarn, we'll just unravel safely to the floor!
And if we chew through the WRONG string?
Gulp.
I can **DO** this! Remember how good I was at Jenga last week?
You LOST, Barry.
C'mon. You guys never trust me to do anything.
Okay, Barry. We...we trust you.
Oh good. Now let me see, the red yarn connects to the yellow yarn, which crosses over the blue... under the orange and loop the loop until...There.

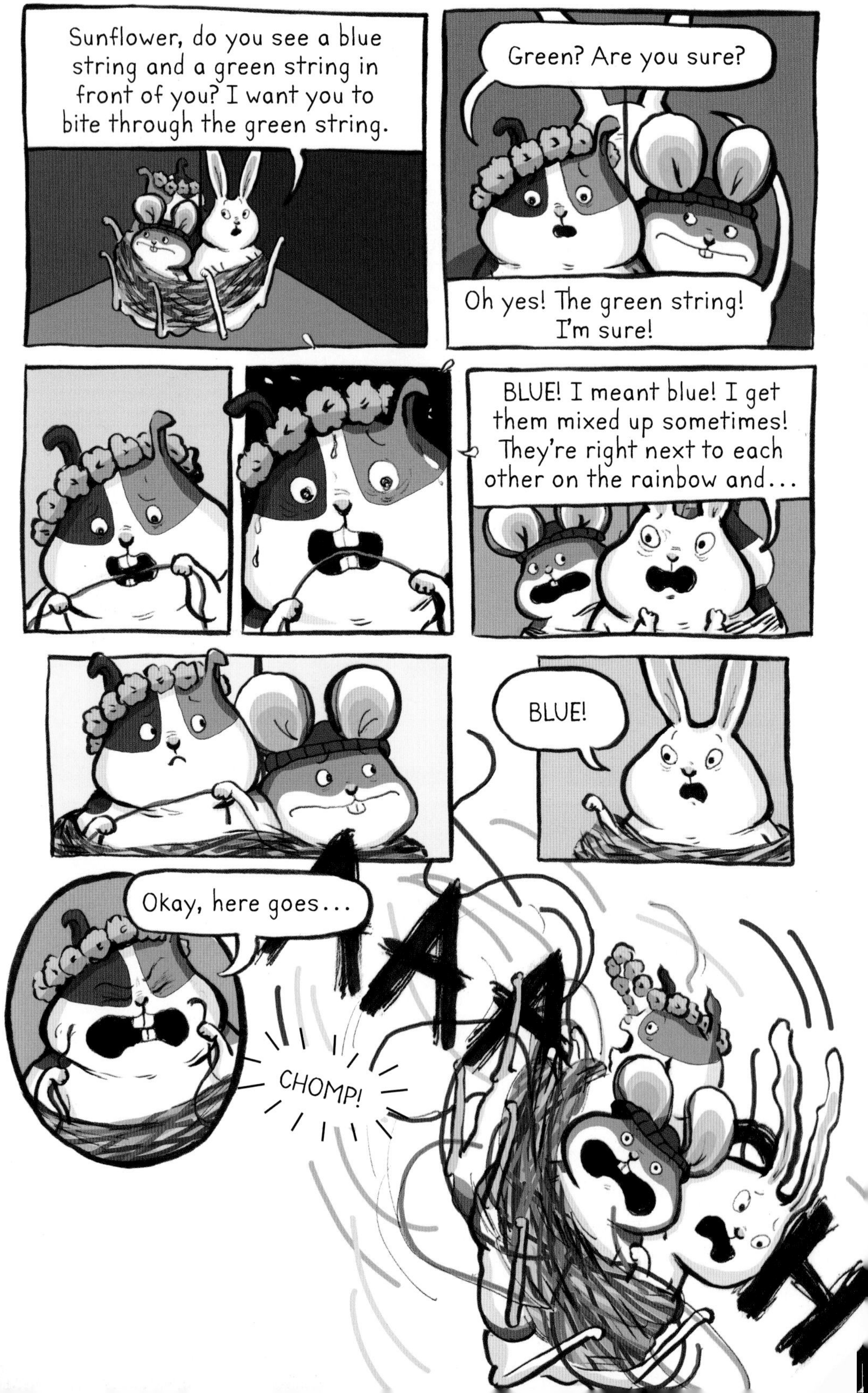
Sunflower, do you see a blue string and a green string in front of you? I want you to bite through the green string.
Green? Are you sure?
Oh yes! The green string! I'm sure!
BLUE! I meant blue! I get them mixed up sometimes! They're right next to each other on the rainbow and...
BLUE!
Okay, here goes...
CHOMP!

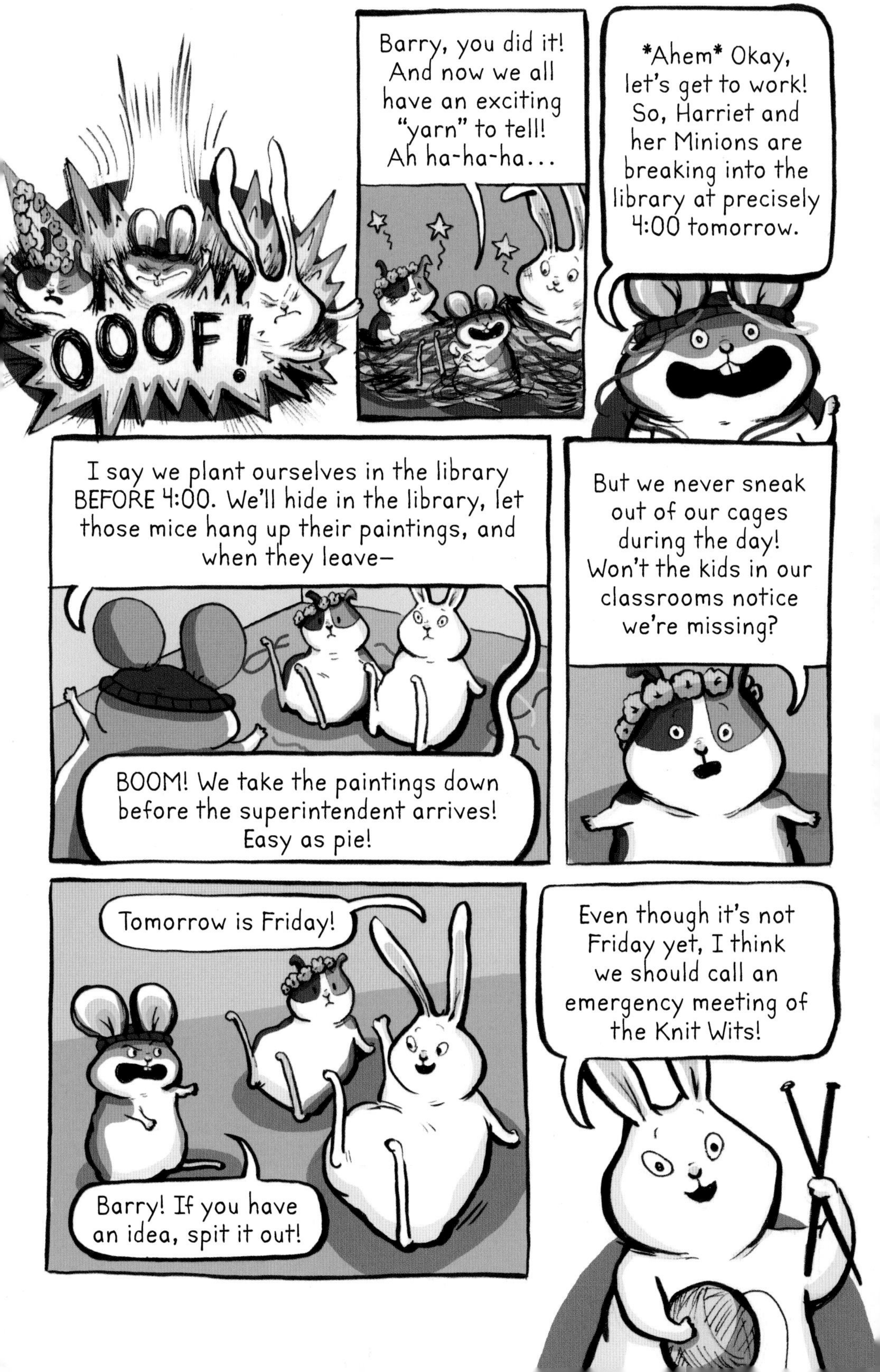
OOOF!
Barry, you did it! And now we all have an exciting "yarn" to tell! Ah ha-ha-ha...
*Ahem* Okay, let's get to work! So, Harriet and her Minions are breaking into the library at precisely 4:00 tomorrow.
I say we plant ourselves in the library BEFORE 4:00. We'll hide in the library, let those mice hang up their paintings, and when they leave—
BOOM! We take the paintings down before the superintendent arrives! Easy as pie!
But we never sneak out of our cages during the day! Won't the kids in our classrooms notice we're missing?
Tomorrow is Friday!
Barry! If you have an idea, spit it out!
Even though it's not Friday yet, I think we should call an emergency meeting of the Knit Wits!

# Chapter 6

This is your second great idea tonight, Barry! You're on a roll!

Thank you!

So we break out of this closet, then we break back IN to our classrooms, plant our body doubles in our cages, then meet in the library, where we'll foil the attempts of Harriet to ruin the art show?

Right! Like I said, easy as pie!

I don't even know how we're going to get out of this closet!

Sometimes the only way OUT is UP!

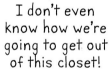

C'mon, let's gather some supplies....

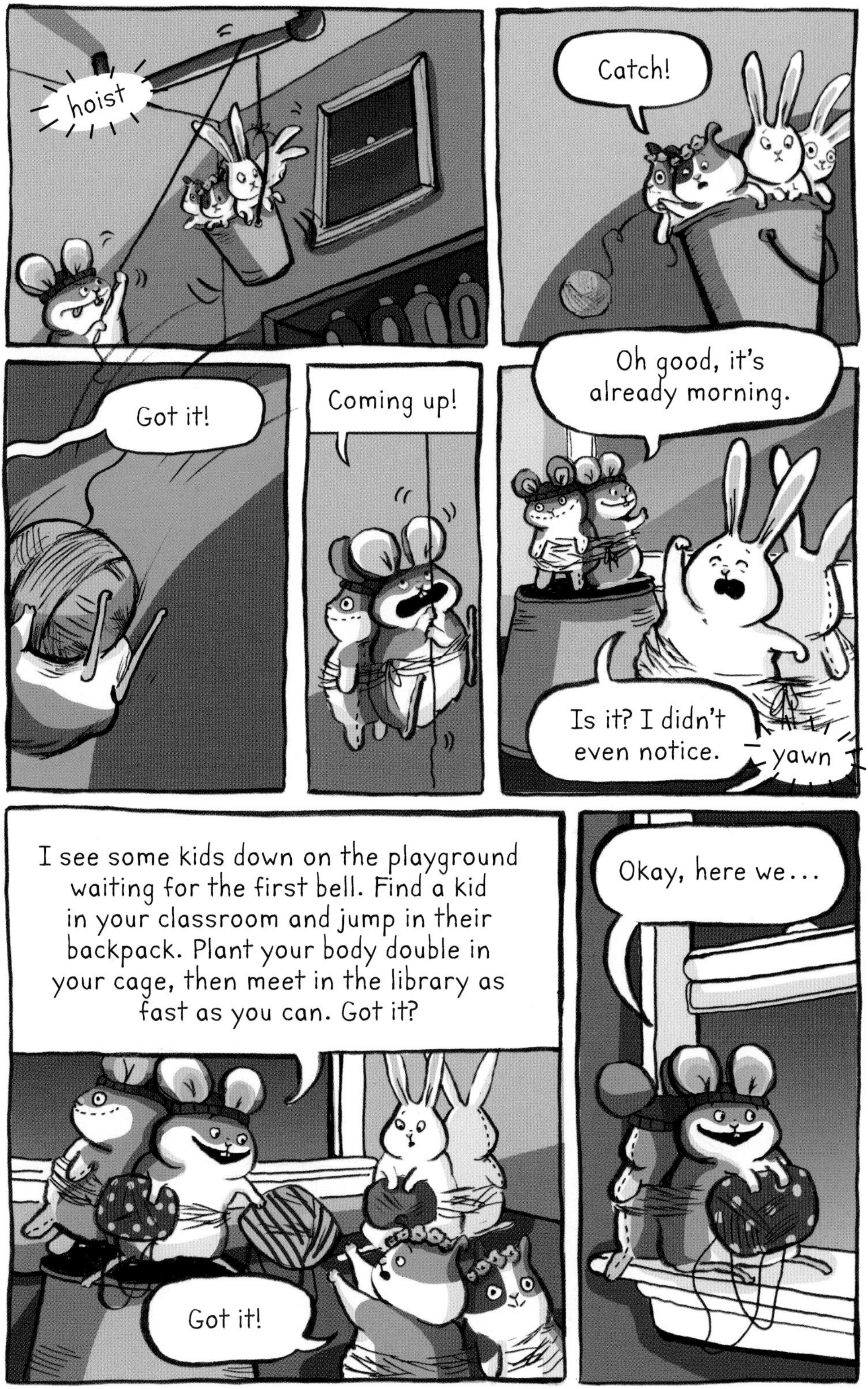
hoist
Catch!
Got it!
Coming up!
Oh good, it's already morning.
Is it? I didn't even notice.
yawn
I see some kids down on the playground waiting for the first bell. Find a kid in your classroom and jump in their backpack. Plant your body double in your cage, then meet in the library as fast as you can. Got it?
Got it!
Okay, here we...

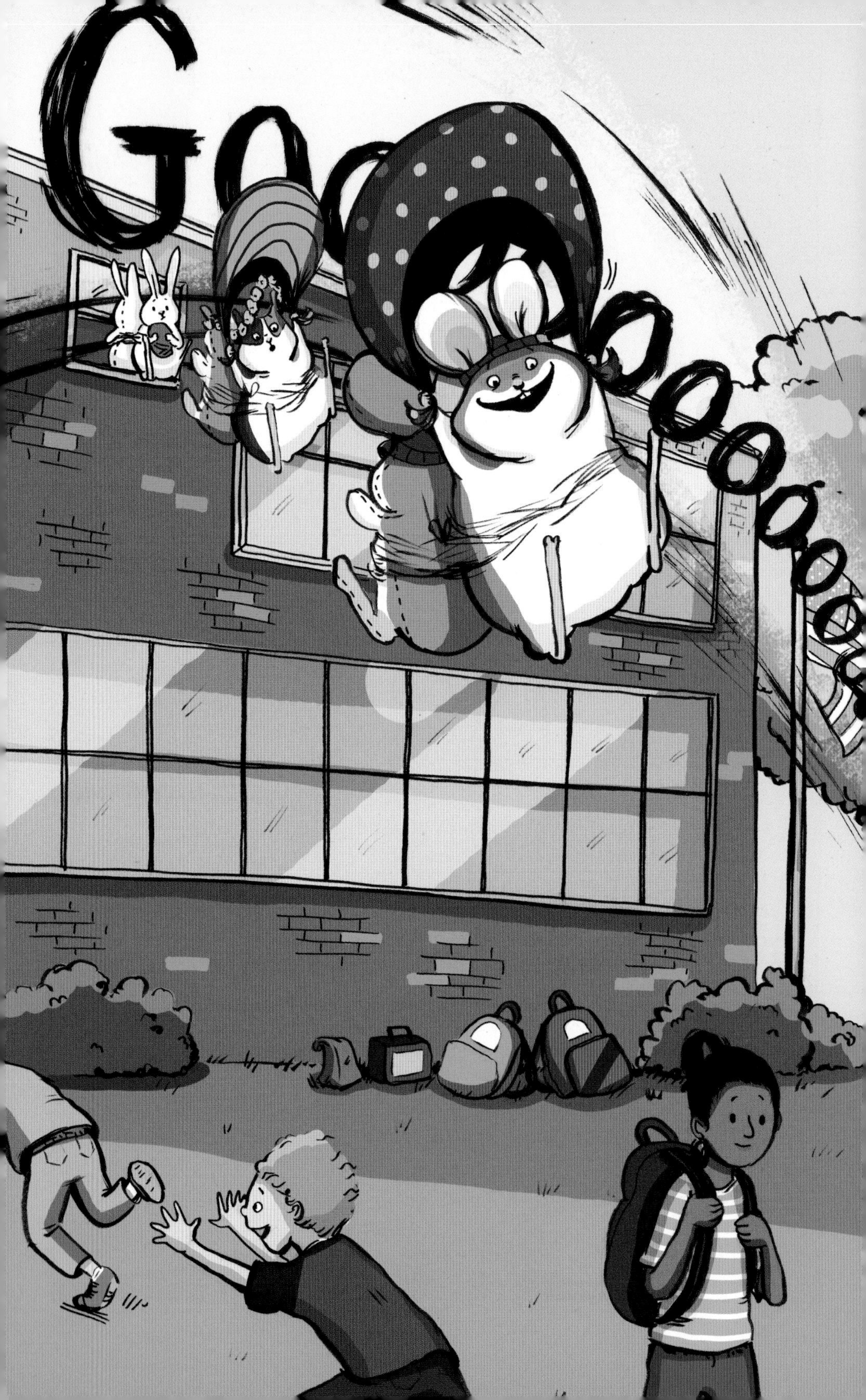
Goooooooooo

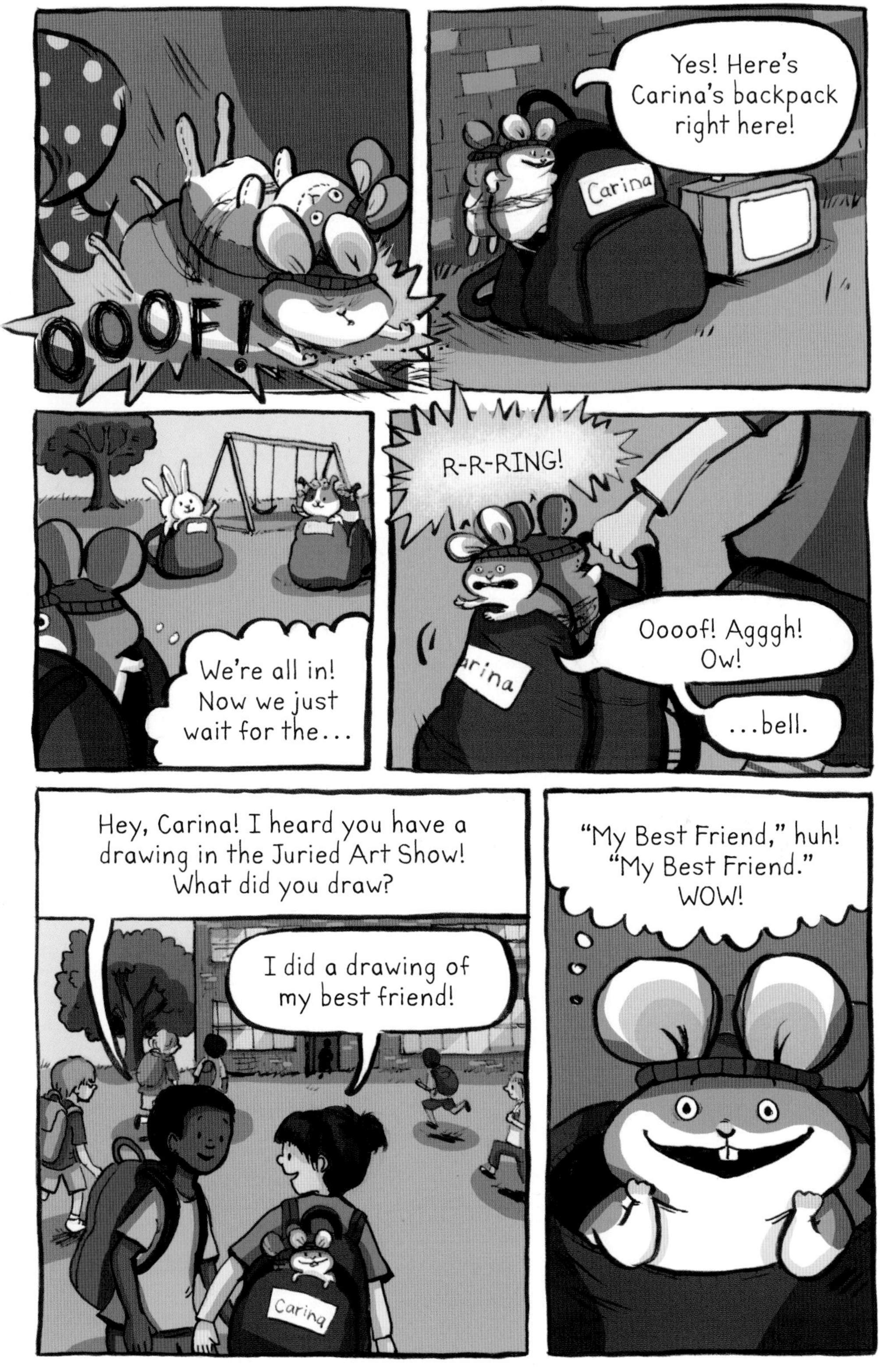
OOOF!
Yes! Here's Carina's backpack right here!
Carina
We're all in! Now we just wait for the...
R-R-RING!
Oooof! Agggh! Ow!
...bell.
Hey, Carina! I heard you have a drawing in the Juried Art Show! What did you draw?
I did a drawing of my best friend!
Carina
"My Best Friend," huh! "My Best Friend." WOW!

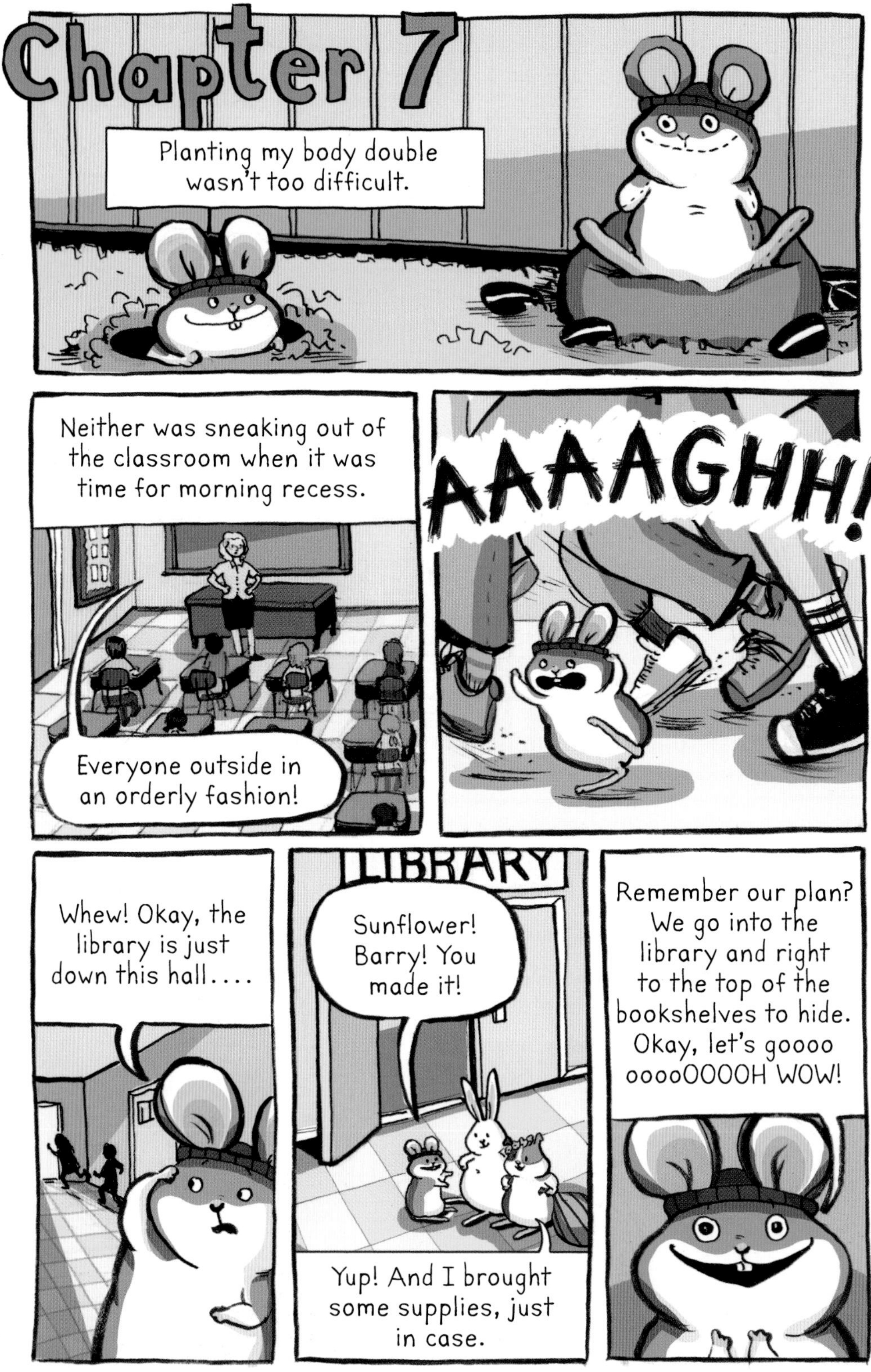
Chapter 7
Planting my body double wasn't too difficult.
Neither was sneaking out of the classroom when it was time for morning recess.
Everyone outside in an orderly fashion!
AAAAGHH!
Whew! Okay, the library is just down this hall....
LIBRARY
Sunflower! Barry! You made it!
Yup! And I brought some supplies, just in case.
Remember our plan? We go into the library and right to the top of the bookshelves to hide. Okay, let's goooo ooooOOOOH WOW!

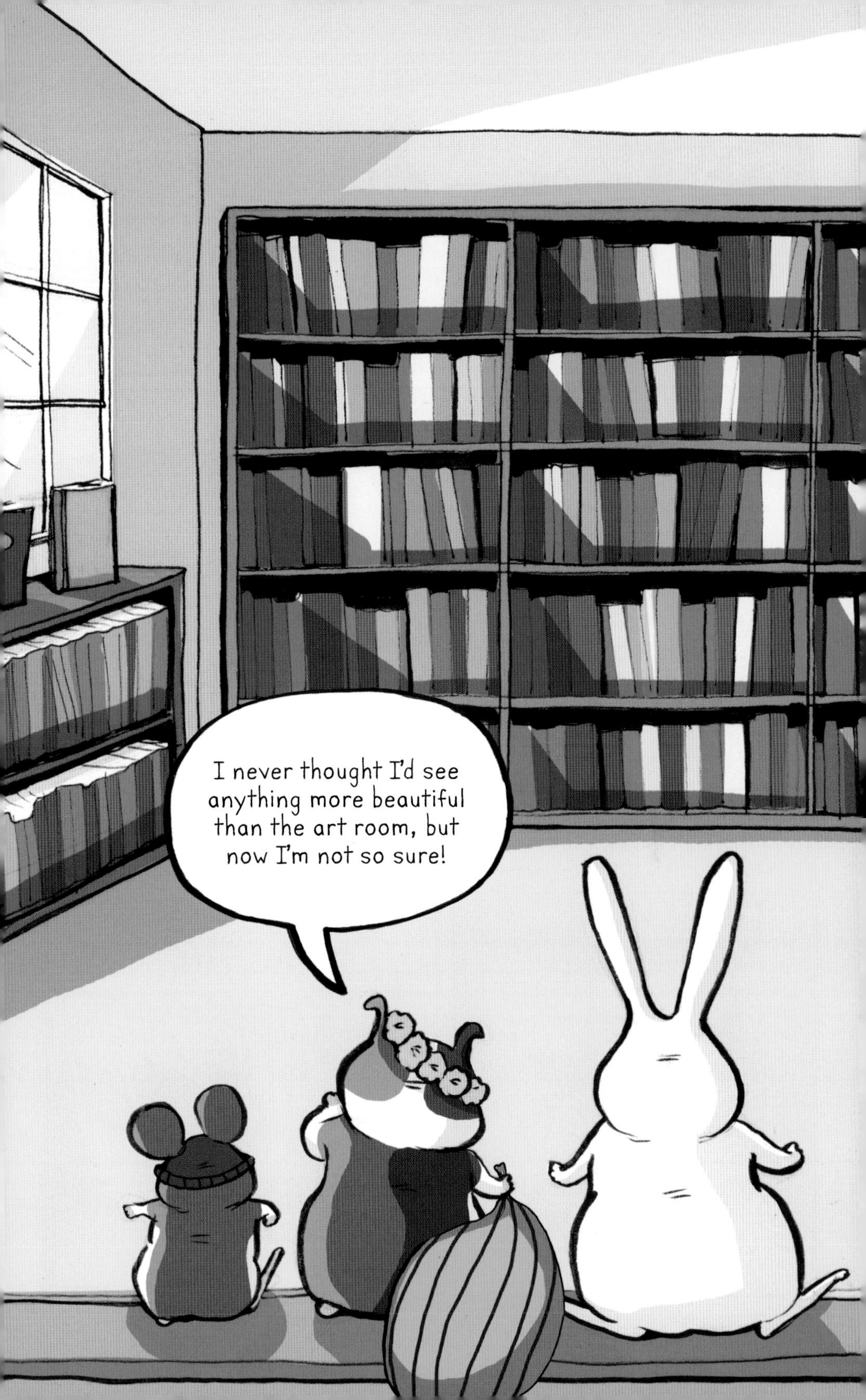
I never thought I'd see anything more beautiful than the art room, but now I'm not so sure!

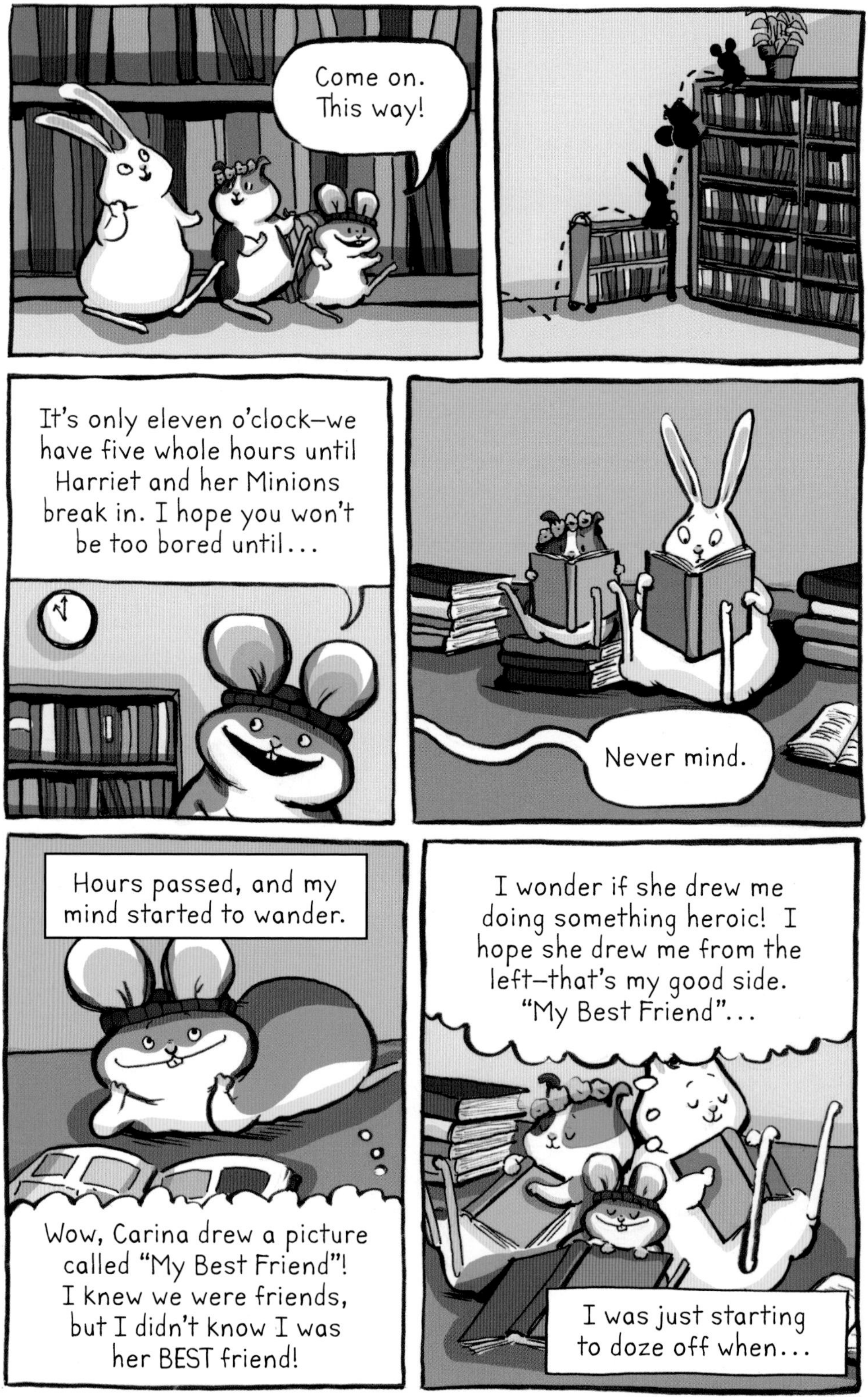

Come on. This way!
It's only eleven o'clock—we have five whole hours until Harriet and her Minions break in. I hope you won't be too bored until...
Never mind.
Hours passed, and my mind started to wander.
Wow, Carina drew a picture called "My Best Friend"! I knew we were friends, but I didn't know I was her BEST friend!
I wonder if she drew me doing something heroic! I hope she drew me from the left—that's my good side. "My Best Friend"...
I was just starting to doze off when...

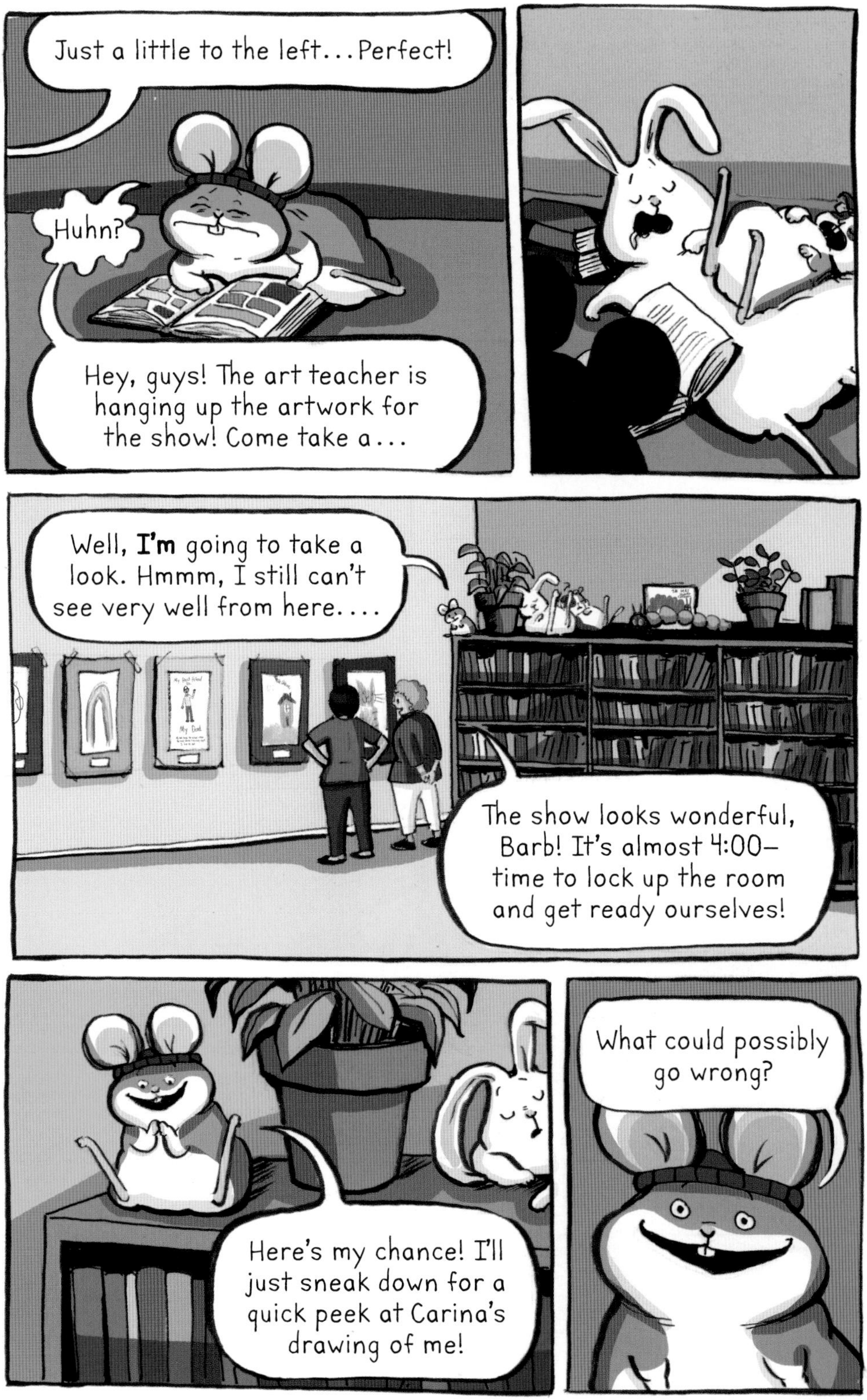
Just a little to the left...Perfect!
Huhn?
Hey, guys! The art teacher is hanging up the artwork for the show! Come take a...
Well, **I'm** going to take a look. Hmmm, I still can't see very well from here....
The show looks wonderful, Barb! It's almost 4:00– time to lock up the room and get ready ourselves!
Here's my chance! I'll just sneak down for a quick peek at Carina's drawing of me!
What could possibly go wrong?

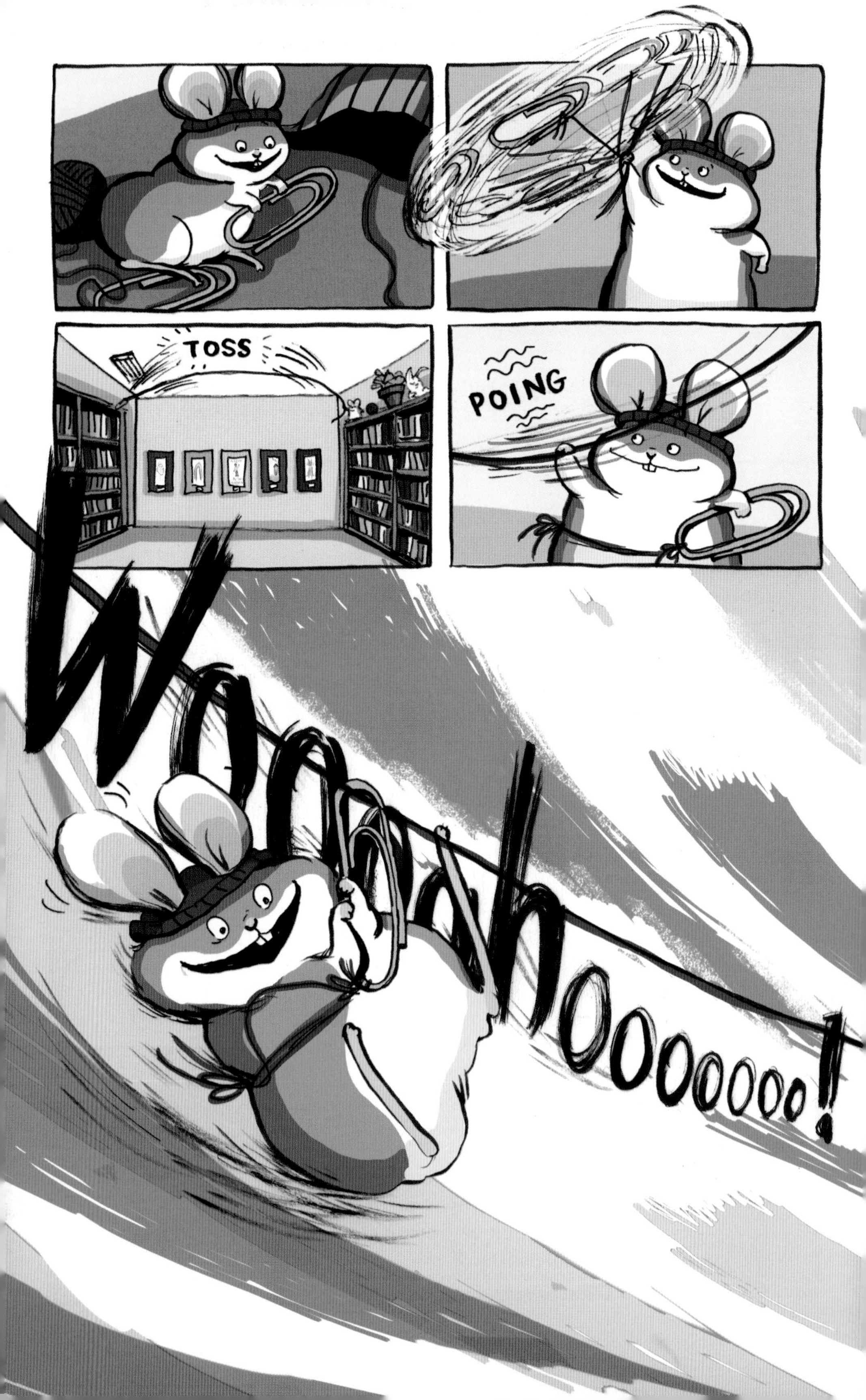
TOSS
POING
Wooahhoooooooo!

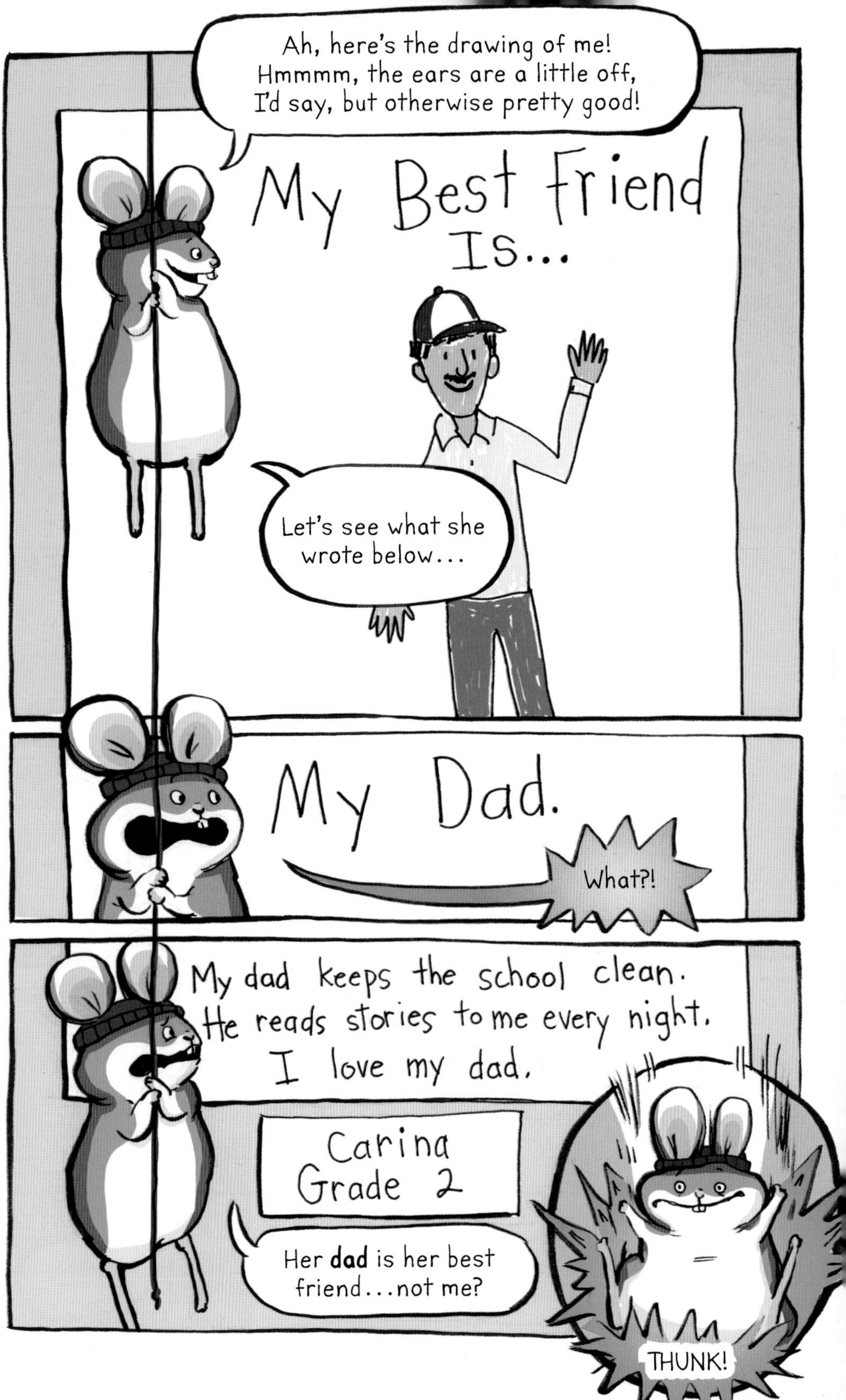

Ah, here's the drawing of me! Hmmmm, the ears are a little off, I'd say, but otherwise pretty good!
My Best Friend Is...
Let's see what she wrote below...
My Dad.
What?!
My dad keeps the school clean. He reads stories to me every night. I love my dad.
Carina Grade 2
Her **dad** is her best friend...not me?
THUNK!

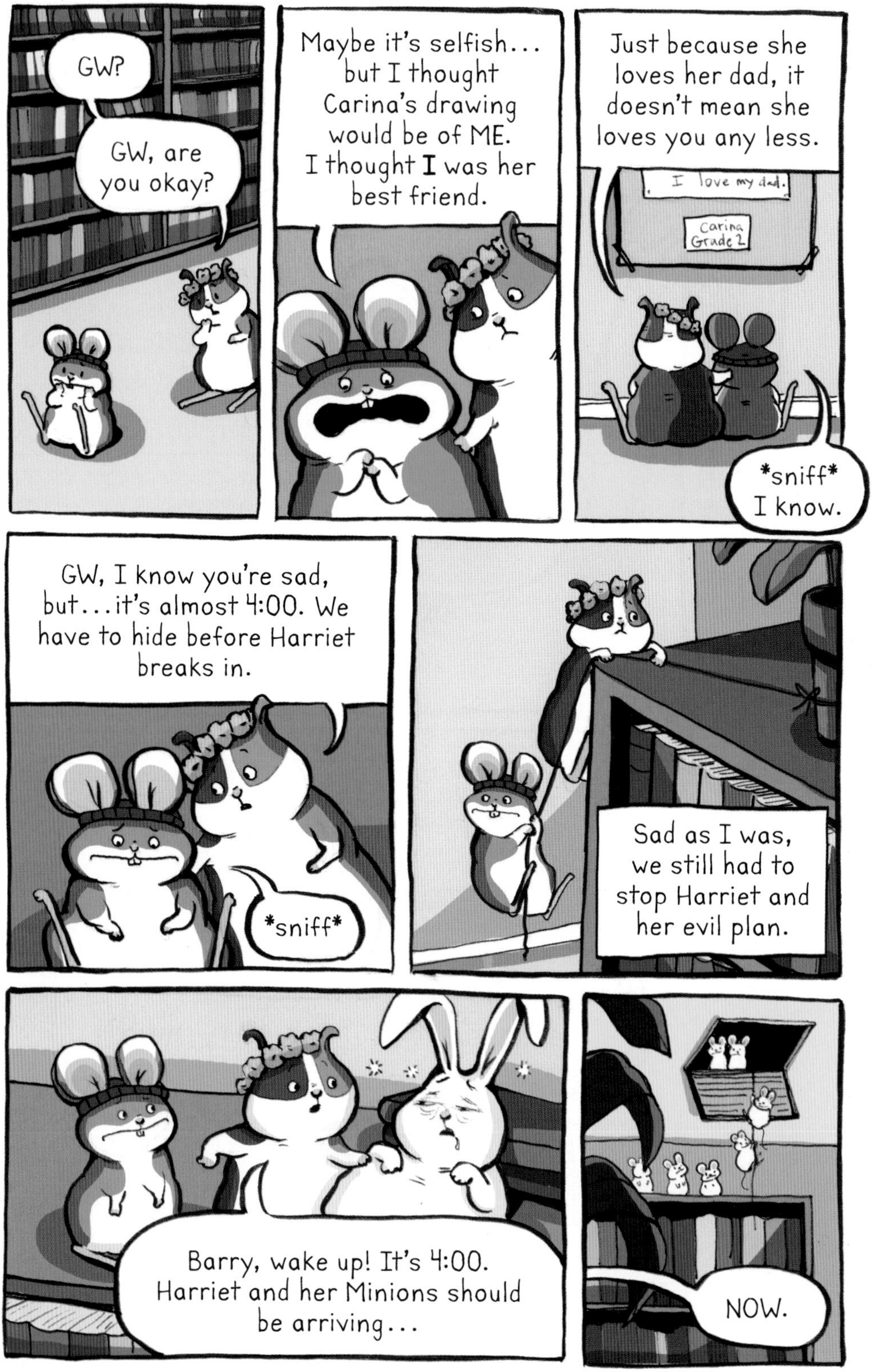
GW?
GW, are you okay?
Maybe it's selfish... but I thought Carina's drawing would be of ME. I thought **I** was her best friend.
Just because she loves her dad, it doesn't mean she loves you any less.
I love my dad.
Carina Grade 2
*sniff* I know.
GW, I know you're sad, but...it's almost 4:00. We have to hide before Harriet breaks in.
*sniff*
Sad as I was, we still had to stop Harriet and her evil plan.
Barry, wake up! It's 4:00. Harriet and her Minions should be arriving...
NOW.

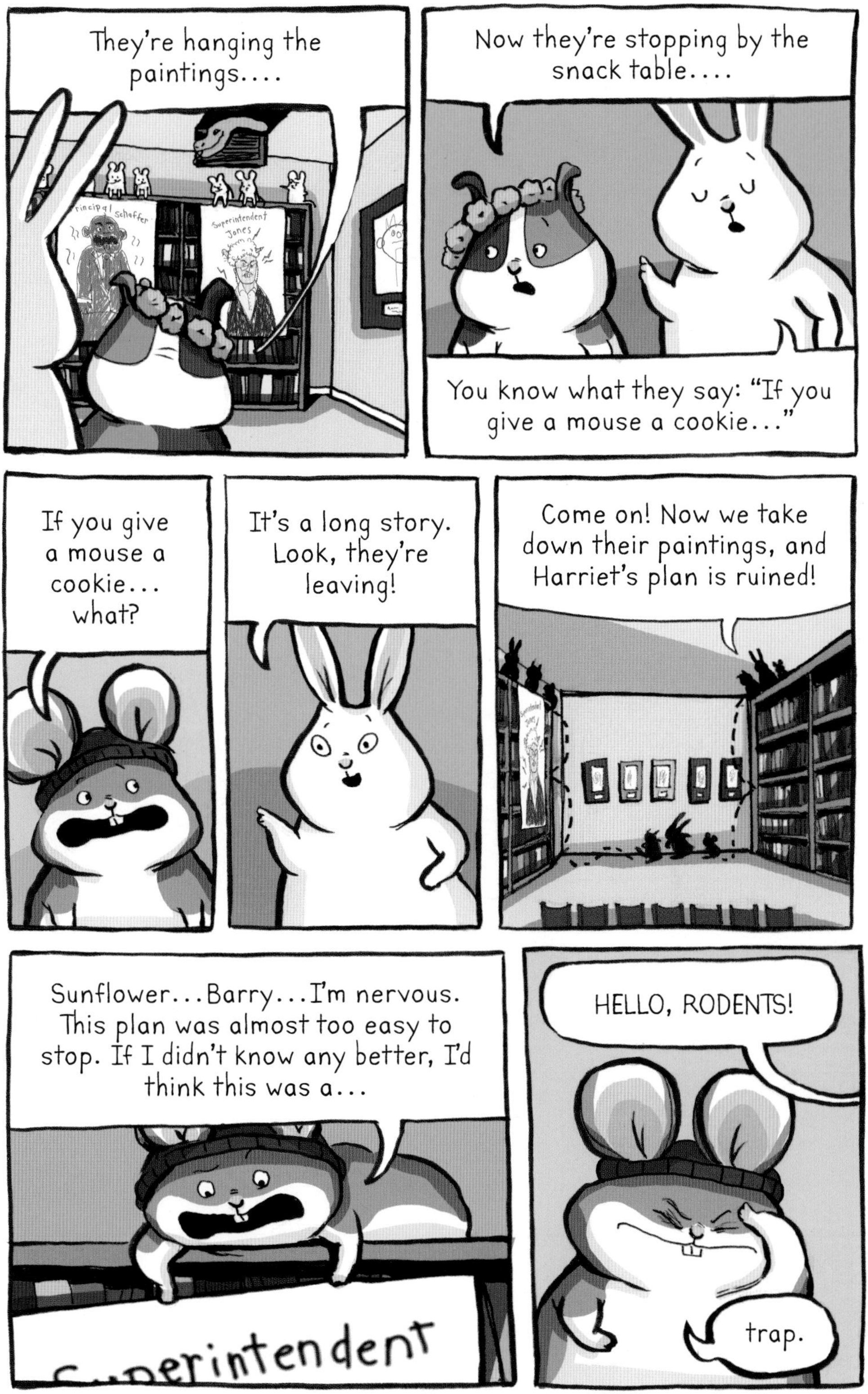
They're hanging the paintings....
Principal Schaffer
Superintendent Jones
Now they're stopping by the snack table....
You know what they say: "If you give a mouse a cookie..."
If you give a mouse a cookie... what?
It's a long story. Look, they're leaving!
Come on! Now we take down their paintings, and Harriet's plan is ruined!
Sunflower...Barry...I'm nervous. This plan was almost too easy to stop. If I didn't know any better, I'd think this was a...
Superintendent
HELLO, RODENTS!
trap.

# Chapter 8

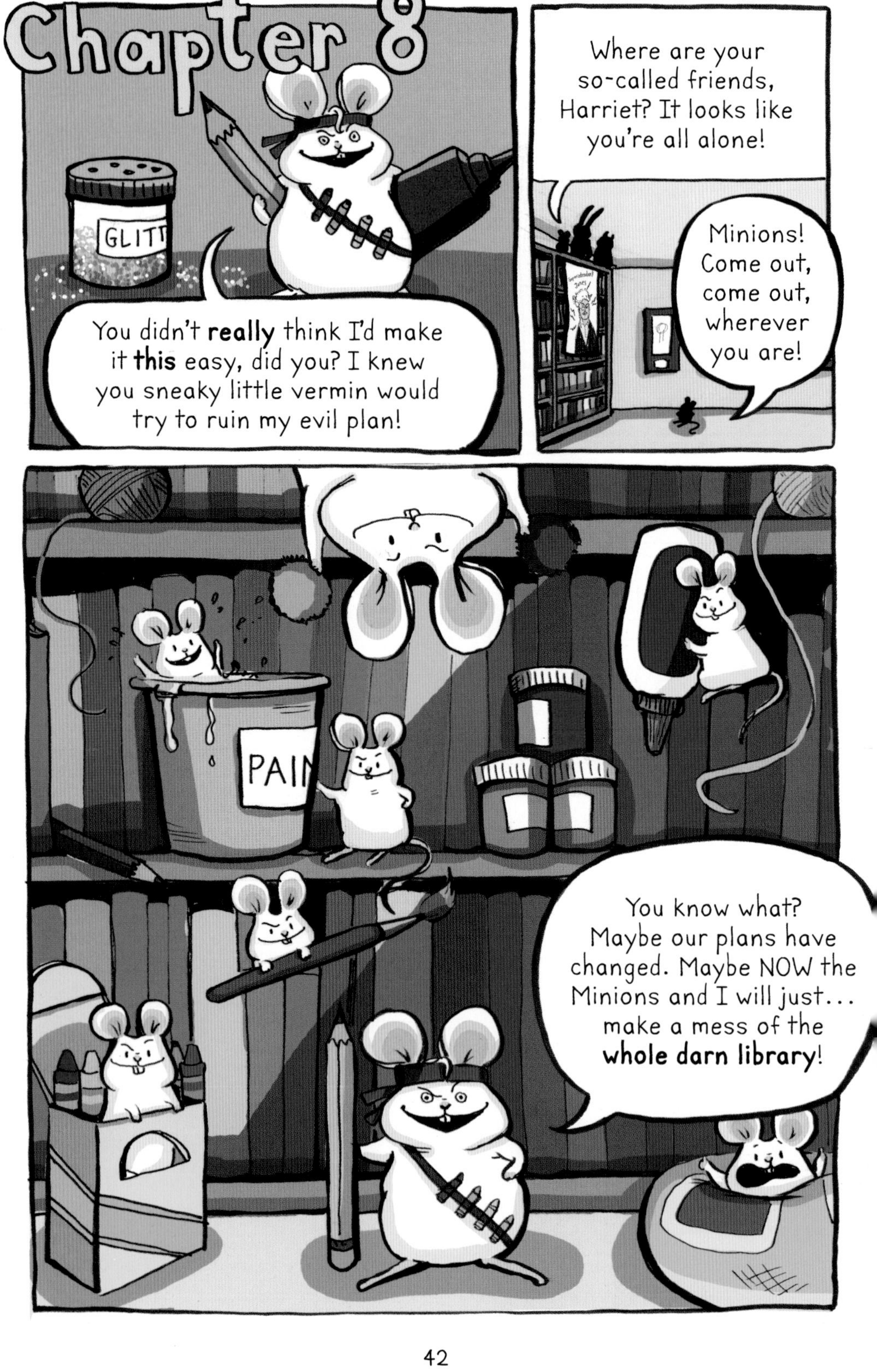
GLITT
You didn't **really** think I'd make it **this** easy, did you? I knew you sneaky little vermin would try to ruin my evil plan!
Where are your so-called friends, Harriet? It looks like you're all alone!
Minions! Come out, come out, wherever you are!
PAIN
You know what? Maybe our plans have changed. Maybe NOW the Minions and I will just... make a mess of the **whole darn library**!

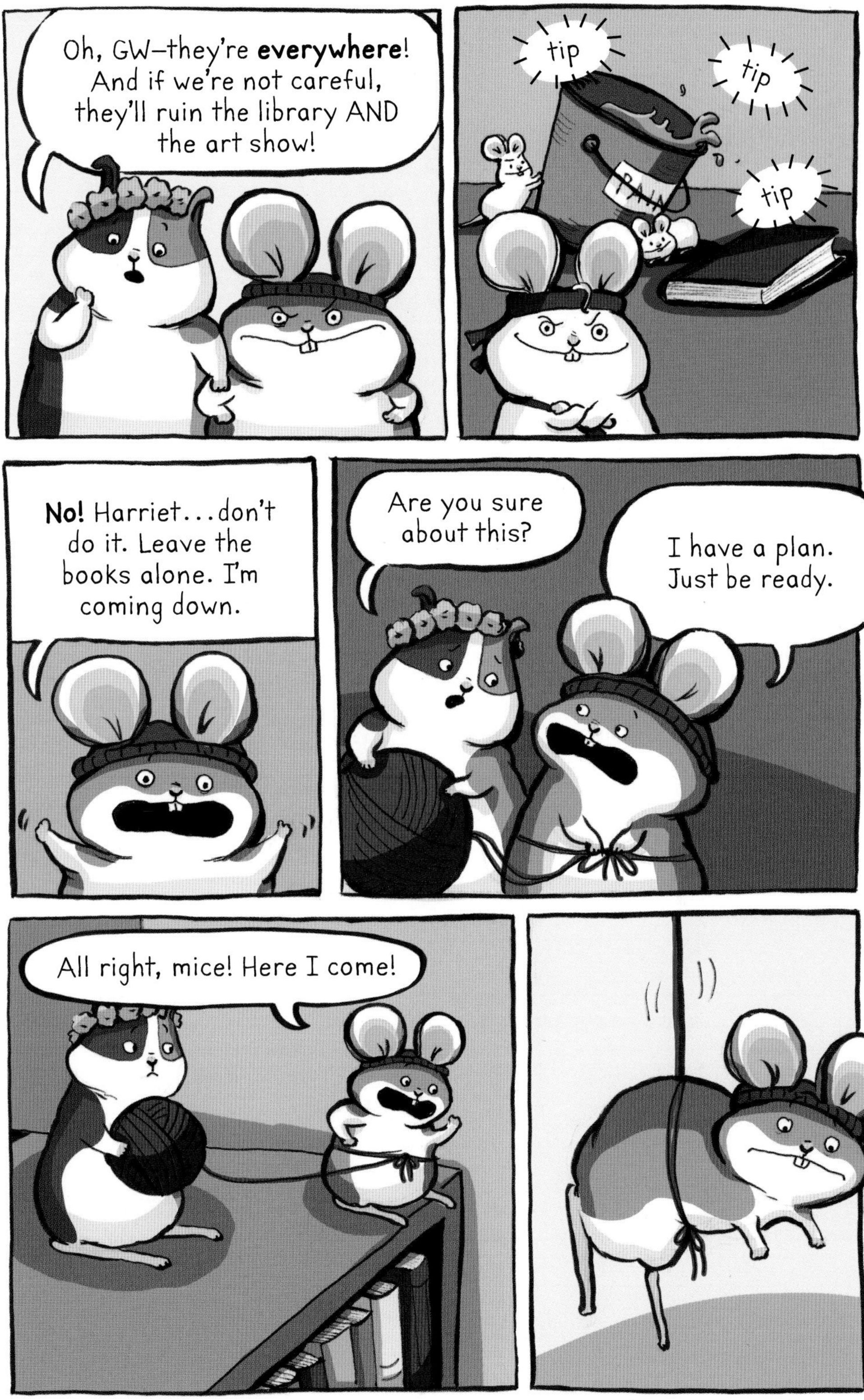
Oh, GW—they're **everywhere**! And if we're not careful, they'll ruin the library AND the art show!
tip
tip
tip
**No!** Harriet. . . don't do it. Leave the books alone. I'm coming down.
Are you sure about this?
I have a plan. Just be ready.
All right, mice! Here I come!

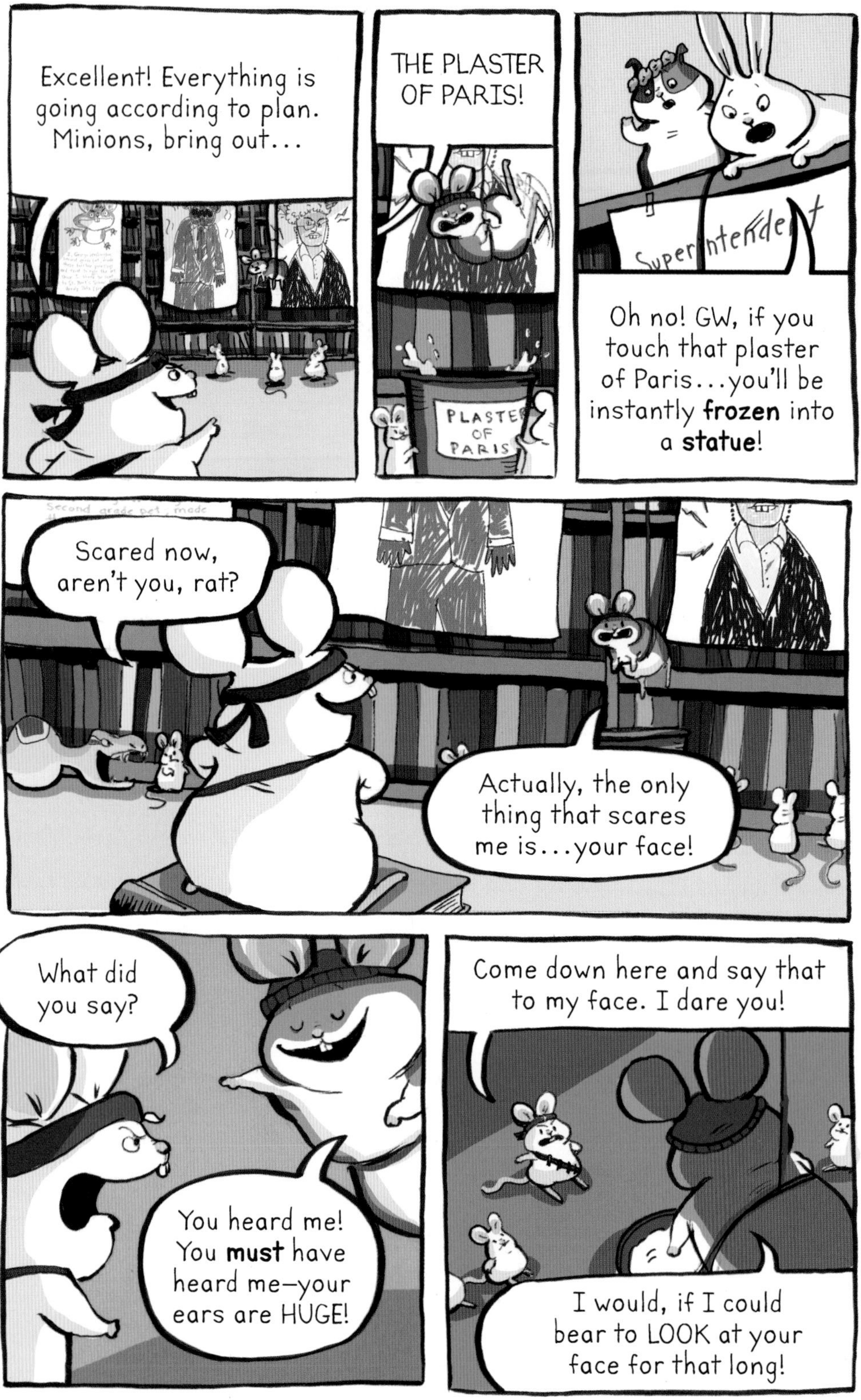
Excellent! Everything is going according to plan. Minions, bring out...
THE PLASTER OF PARIS!
PLASTER OF PARIS
Superintendent
Oh no! GW, if you touch that plaster of Paris...you'll be instantly **frozen** into a **statue**!
Scared now, aren't you, rat?
Actually, the only thing that scares me is...your face!
What did you say?
You heard me! You **must** have heard me—your ears are HUGE!
Come down here and say that to my face. I dare you!
I would, if I could bear to LOOK at your face for that long!

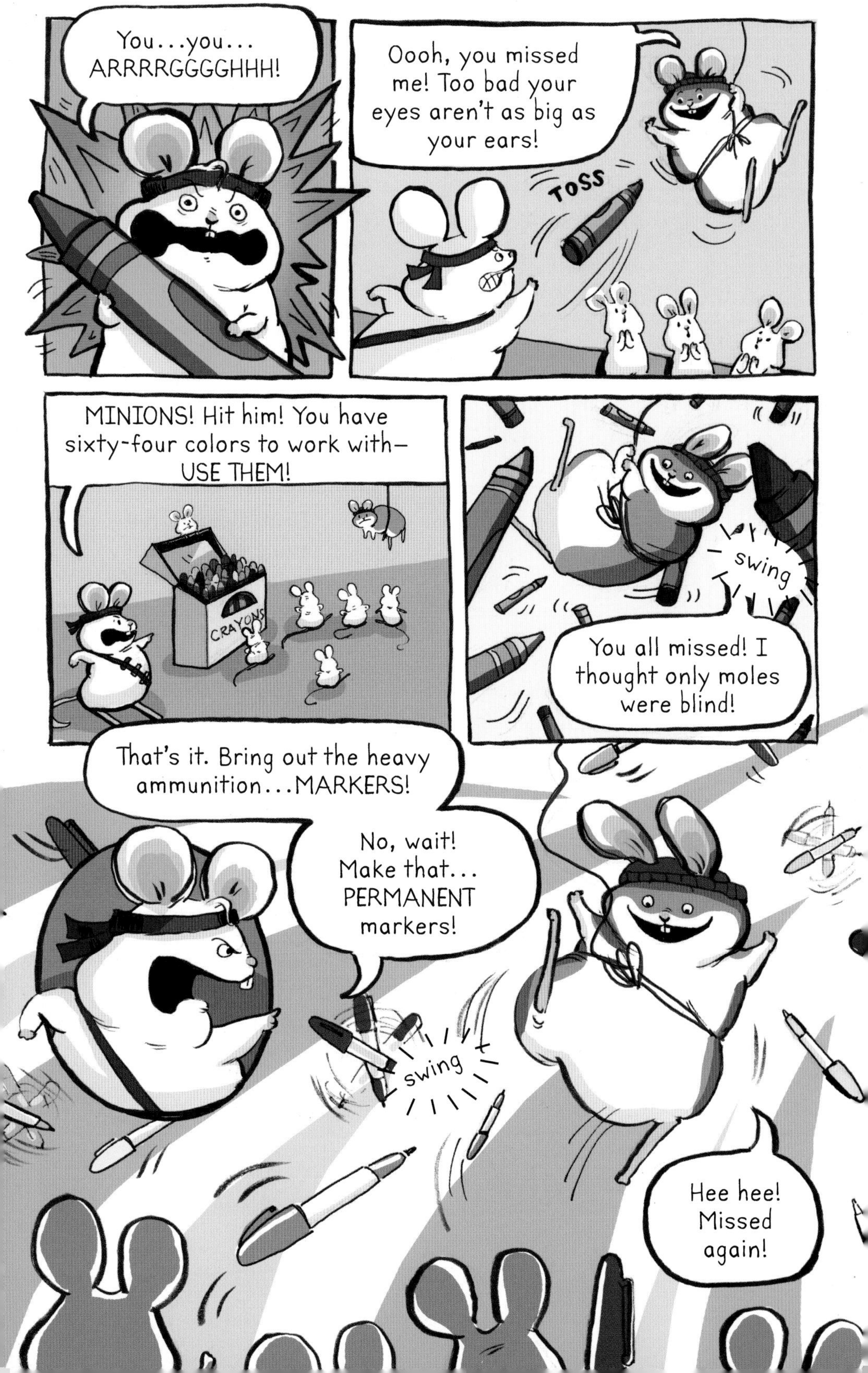
You...you... ARRRRGGGGHHH!
Oooh, you missed me! Too bad your eyes aren't as big as your ears!
TOSS
MINIONS! Hit him! You have sixty-four colors to work with— USE THEM!
CRAYONS
swing
You all missed! I thought only moles were blind!
That's it. Bring out the heavy ammunition...MARKERS!
No, wait! Make that... PERMANENT markers!
swing
Hee hee! Missed again!

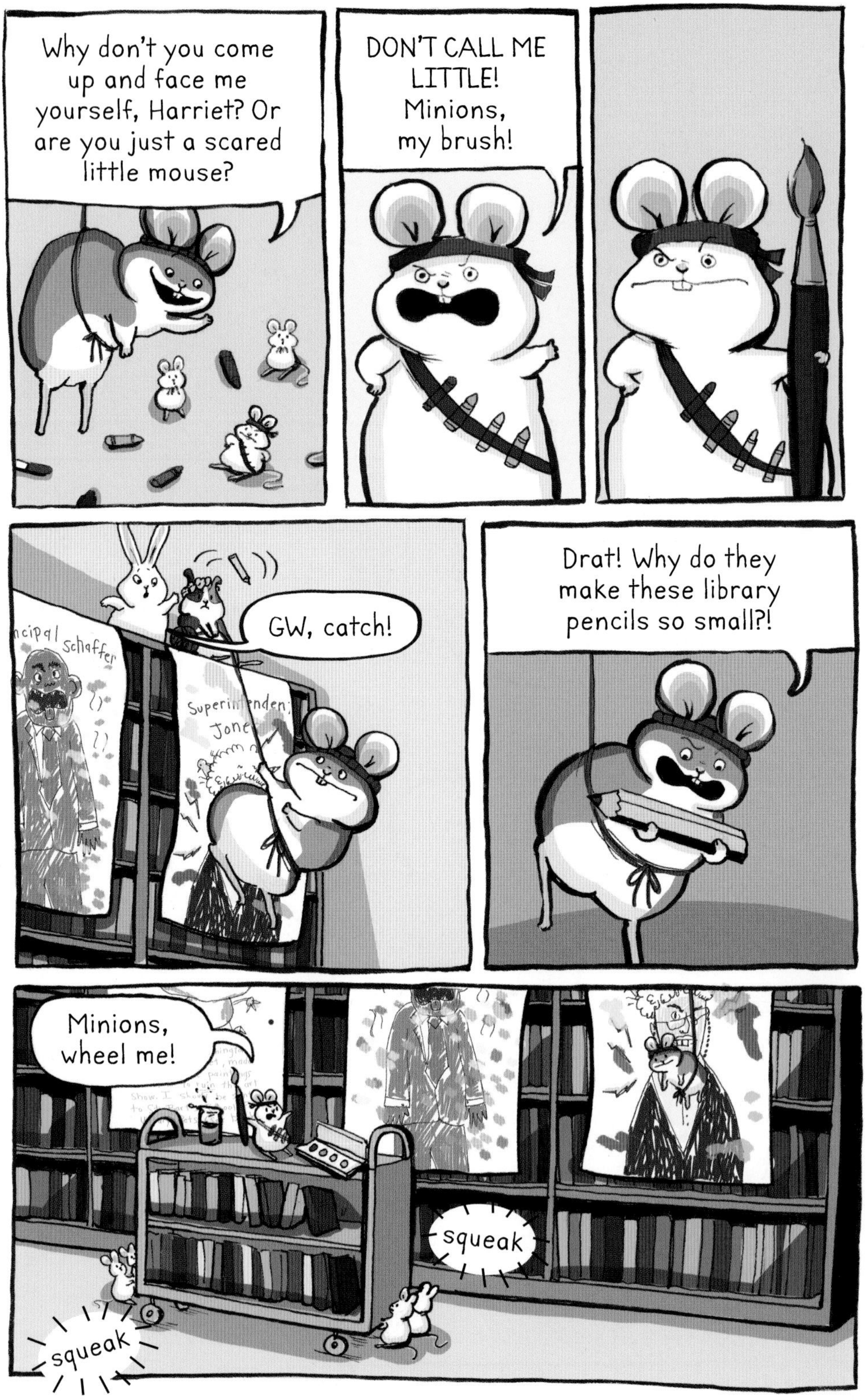
Why don't you come up and face me yourself, Harriet? Or are you just a scared little mouse?
DON'T CALL ME LITTLE! Minions, my brush!
GW, catch!
Drat! Why do they make these library pencils so small?!
Minions, wheel me!
squeak
squeak

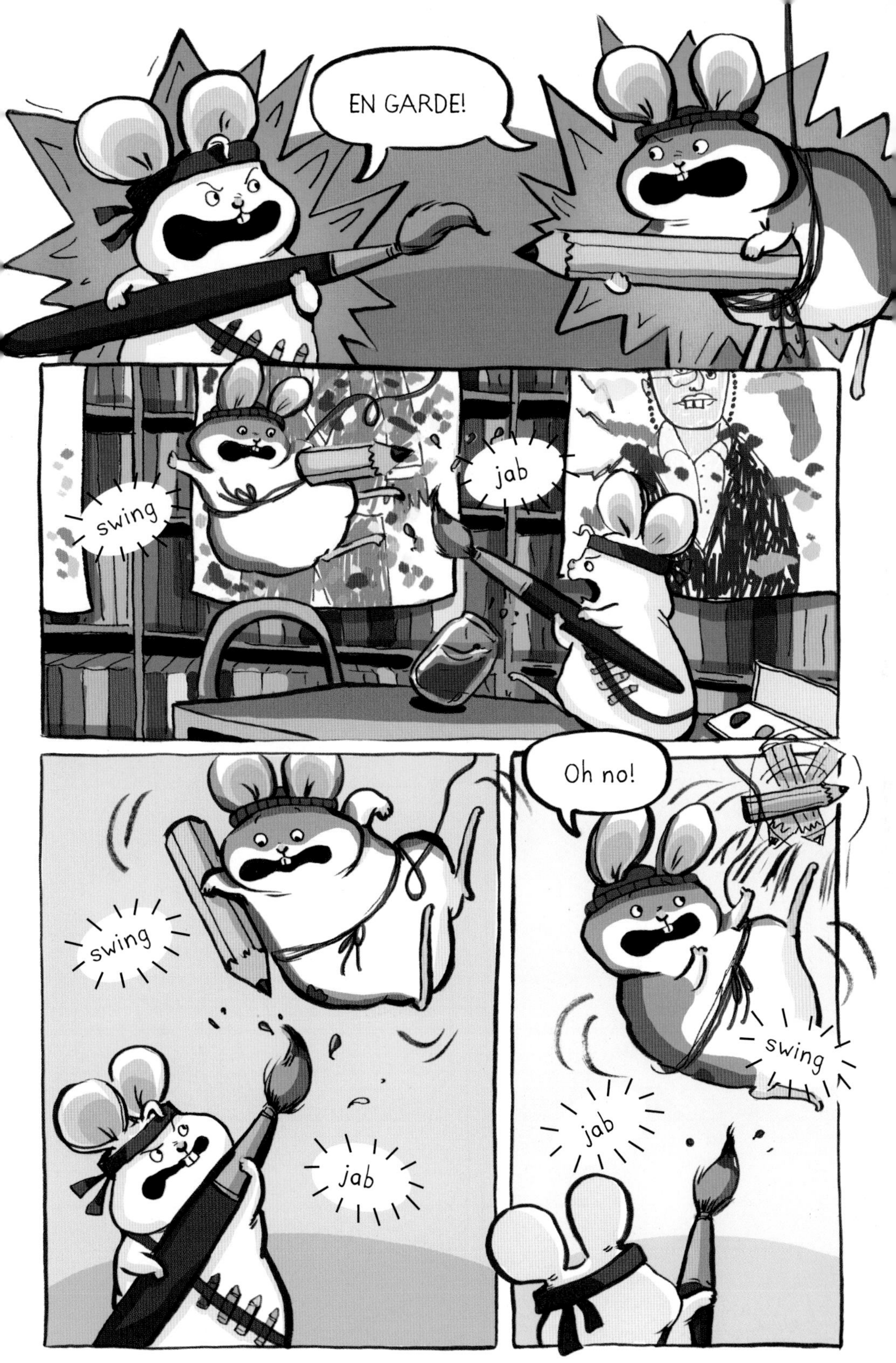
EN GARDE!
swing
jab
swing
jab
Oh no!
jab
swing

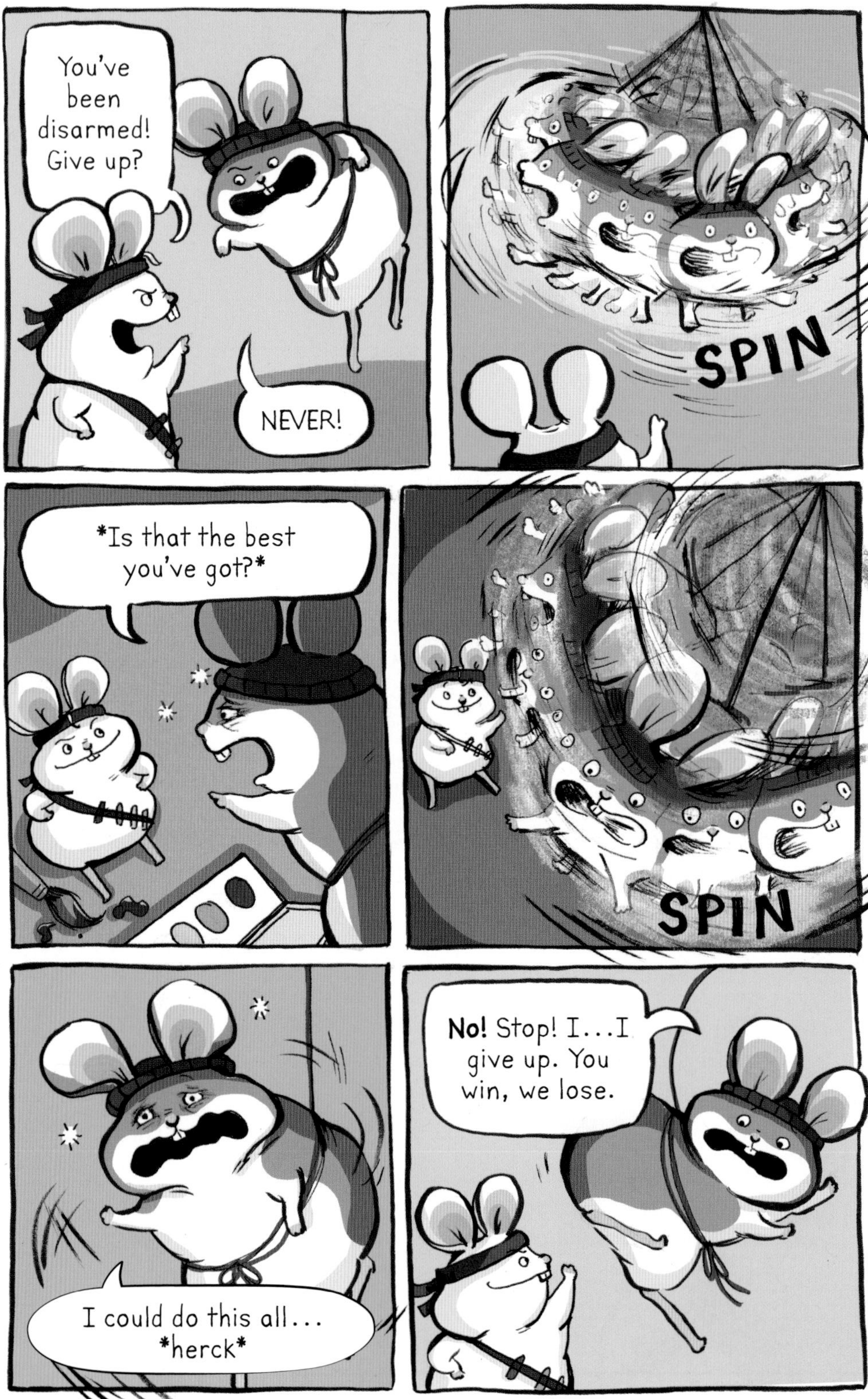
You've been disarmed! Give up?
NEVER!
SPIN
*Is that the best you've got?*
SPIN
I could do this all... *herck*
**No!** Stop! I...I give up. You win, we lose.

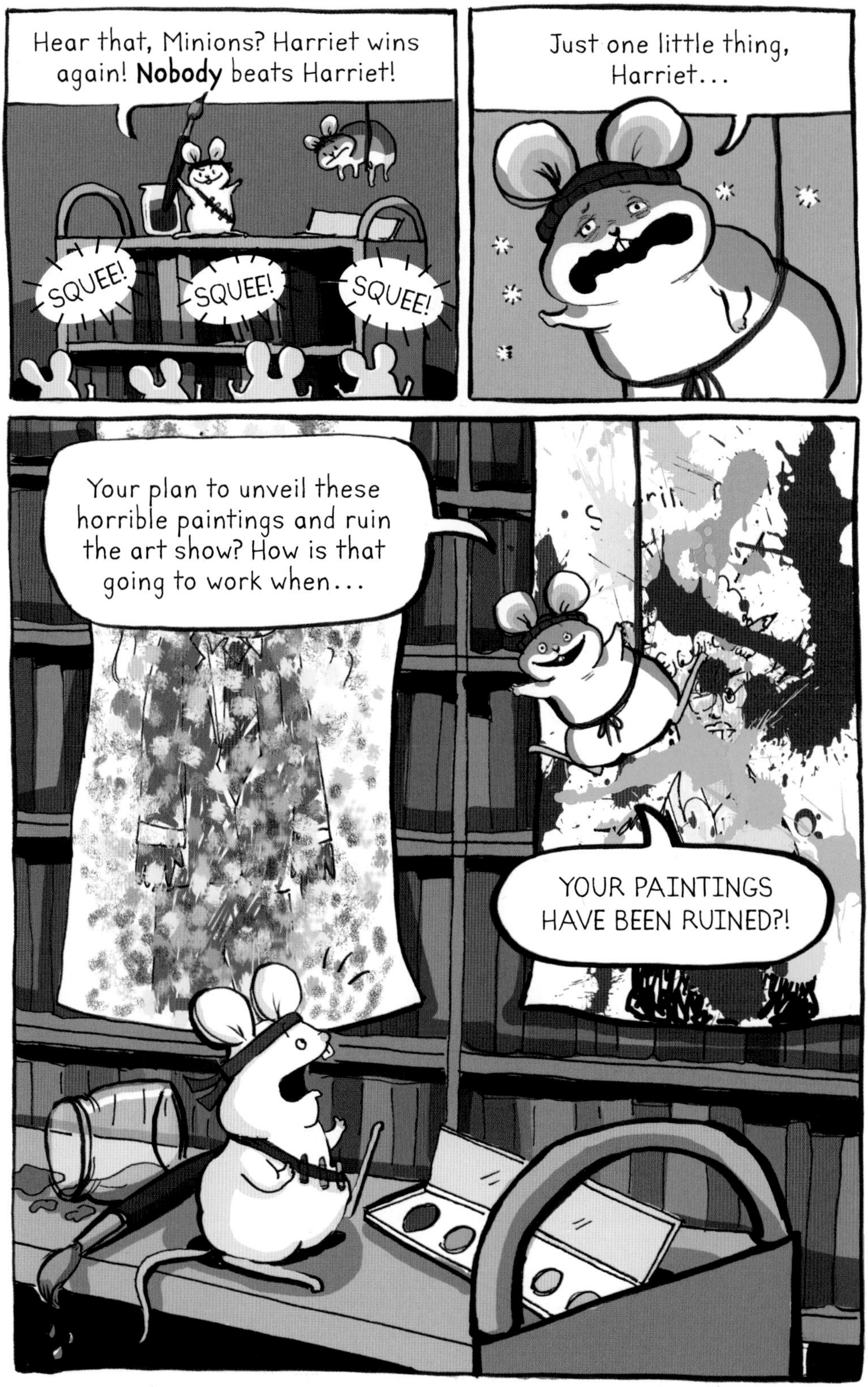
Hear that, Minions? Harriet wins again! **Nobody** beats Harriet!
SQUEE!
SQUEE!
SQUEE!
Just one little thing, Harriet...
Your plan to unveil these horrible paintings and ruin the art show? How is that going to work when...
YOUR PAINTINGS HAVE BEEN RUINED?!

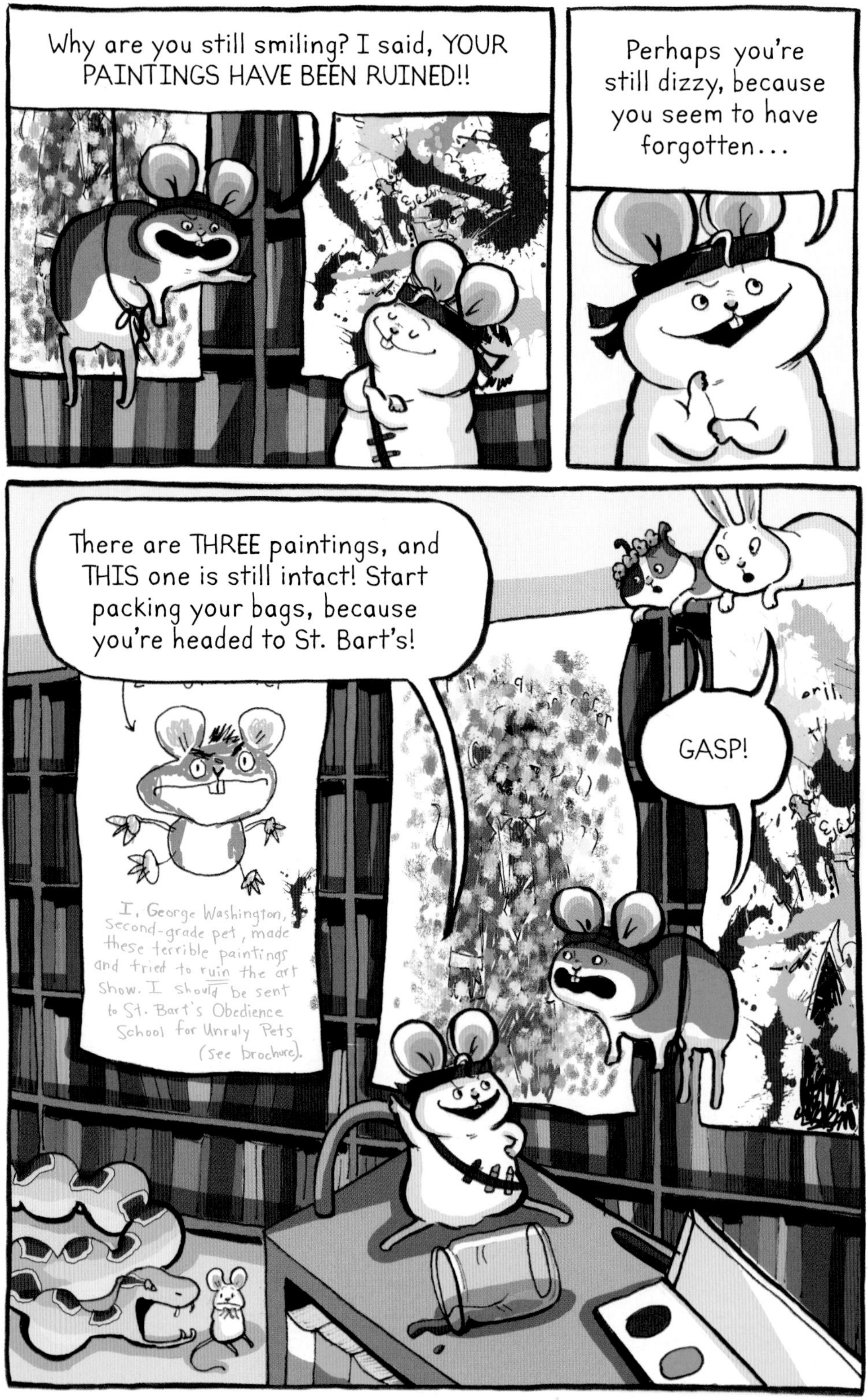
Why are you still smiling? I said, YOUR PAINTINGS HAVE BEEN RUINED!!
Perhaps you're still dizzy, because you seem to have forgotten...
There are THREE paintings, and THIS one is still intact! Start packing your bags, because you're headed to St. Bart's!
I, George Washington, second-grade pet, made these terrible paintings and tried to ruin the art show. I should be sent to St. Bart's Obedience School for Unruly Pets (see brochure).
GASP!

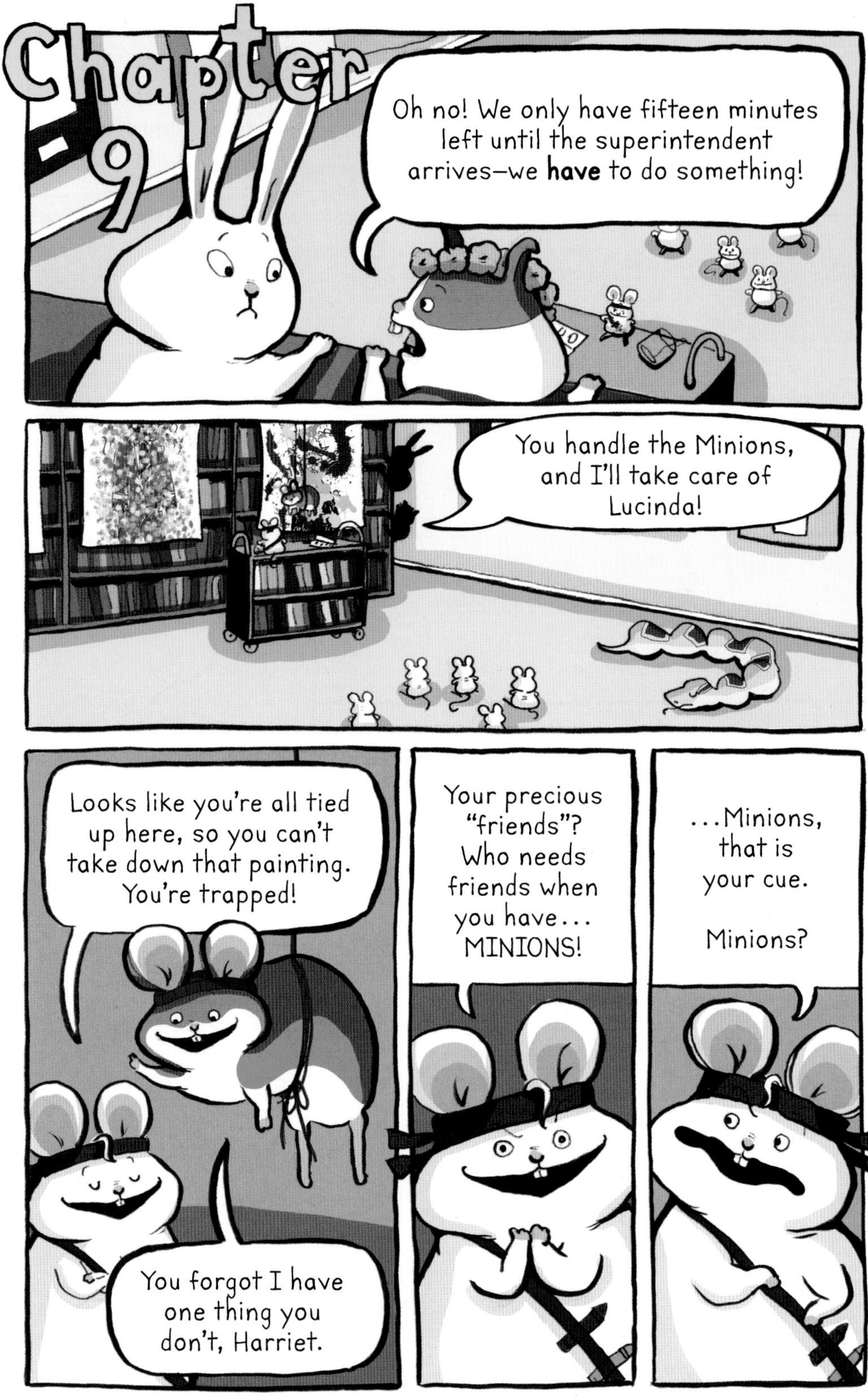
Chapter 9
Oh no! We only have fifteen minutes left until the superintendent arrives—we **have** to do something!
You handle the Minions, and I'll take care of Lucinda!
Looks like you're all tied up here, so you can't take down that painting. You're trapped!
You forgot I have one thing you don't, Harriet.
Your precious "friends"? Who needs friends when you have... MINIONS!
...Minions, that is your cue.
Minions?

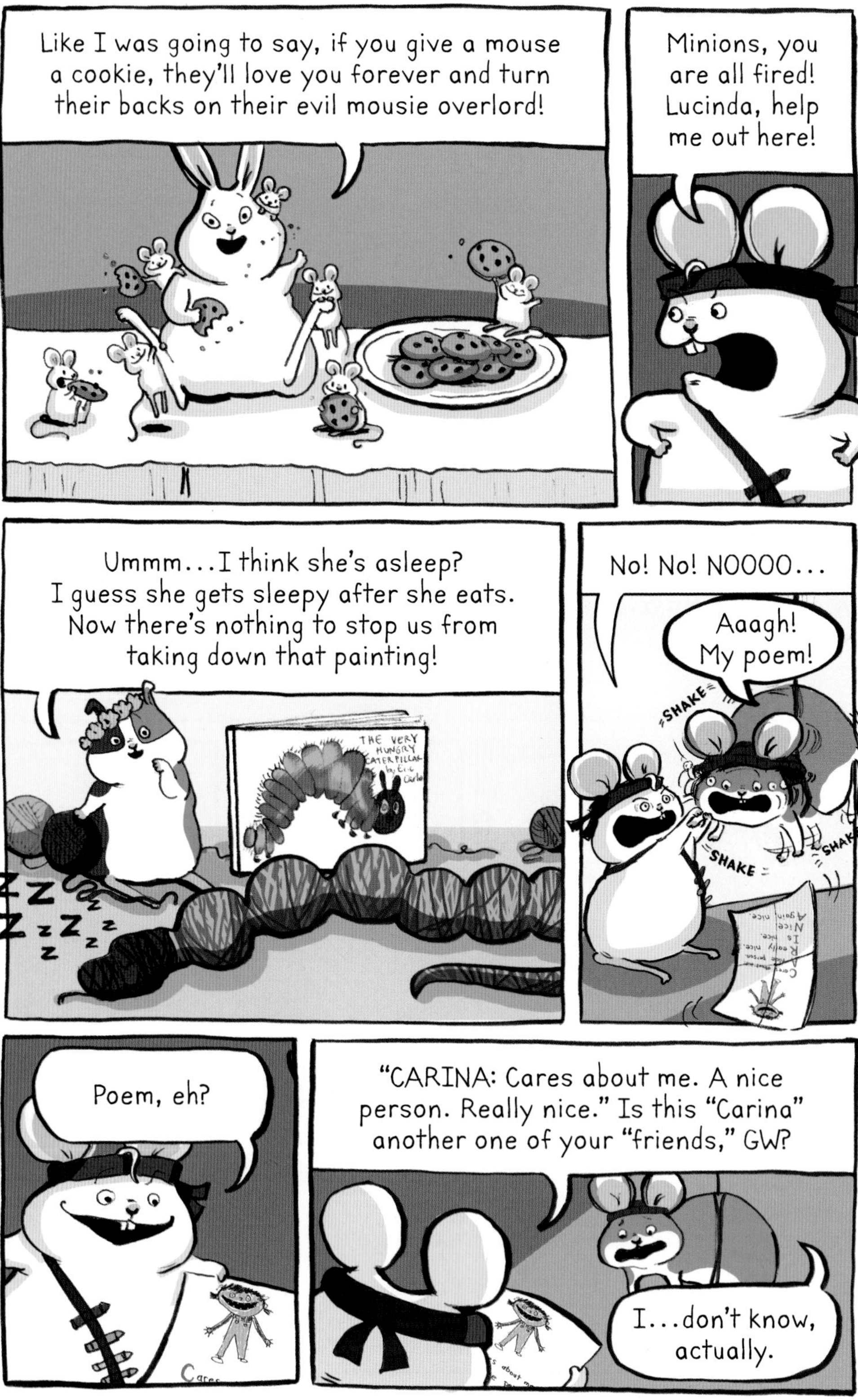
Like I was going to say, if you give a mouse a cookie, they'll love you forever and turn their backs on their evil mousie overlord!
Minions, you are all fired! Lucinda, help me out here!
Ummm...I think she's asleep? I guess she gets sleepy after she eats. Now there's nothing to stop us from taking down that painting!
THE VERY HUNGRY CATERPILLAR
No! No! NOOOO...
Aaagh! My poem!
SHAKE
SHAKE
SHAKE
Poem, eh?
"CARINA: Cares about me. A nice person. Really nice." Is this "Carina" another one of your "friends," GW?
I...don't know, actually.

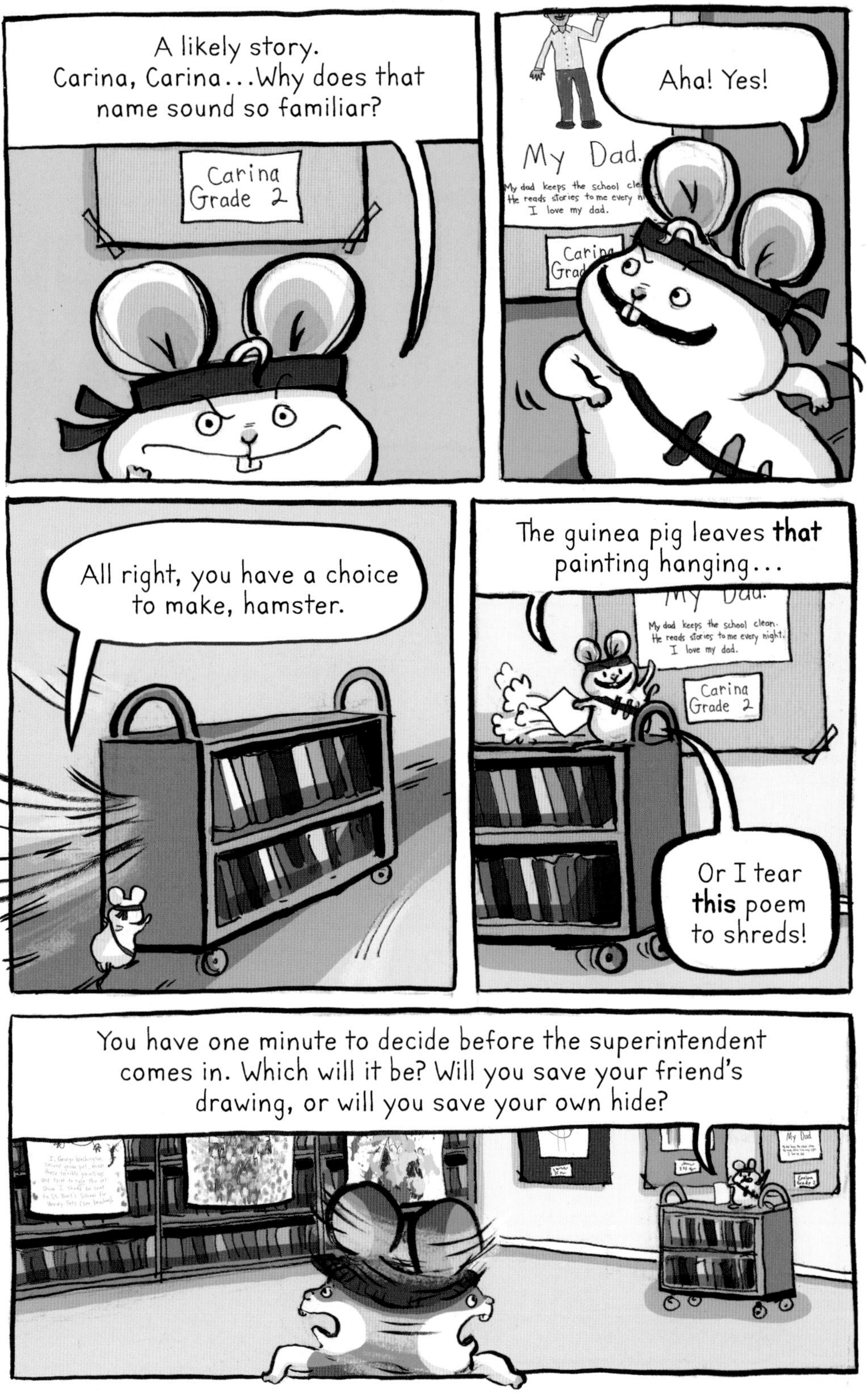
A likely story.
Carina, Carina...Why does that name sound so familiar?
Carina
Grade 2
Aha! Yes!
My Dad.
All right, you have a choice to make, hamster.
The guinea pig leaves **that** painting hanging...
My dad keeps the school clean.
He reads stories to me every night.
I love my dad.
Carina
Grade 2
Or I tear **this** poem to shreds!
You have one minute to decide before the superintendent comes in. Which will it be? Will you save your friend's drawing, or will you save your own hide?

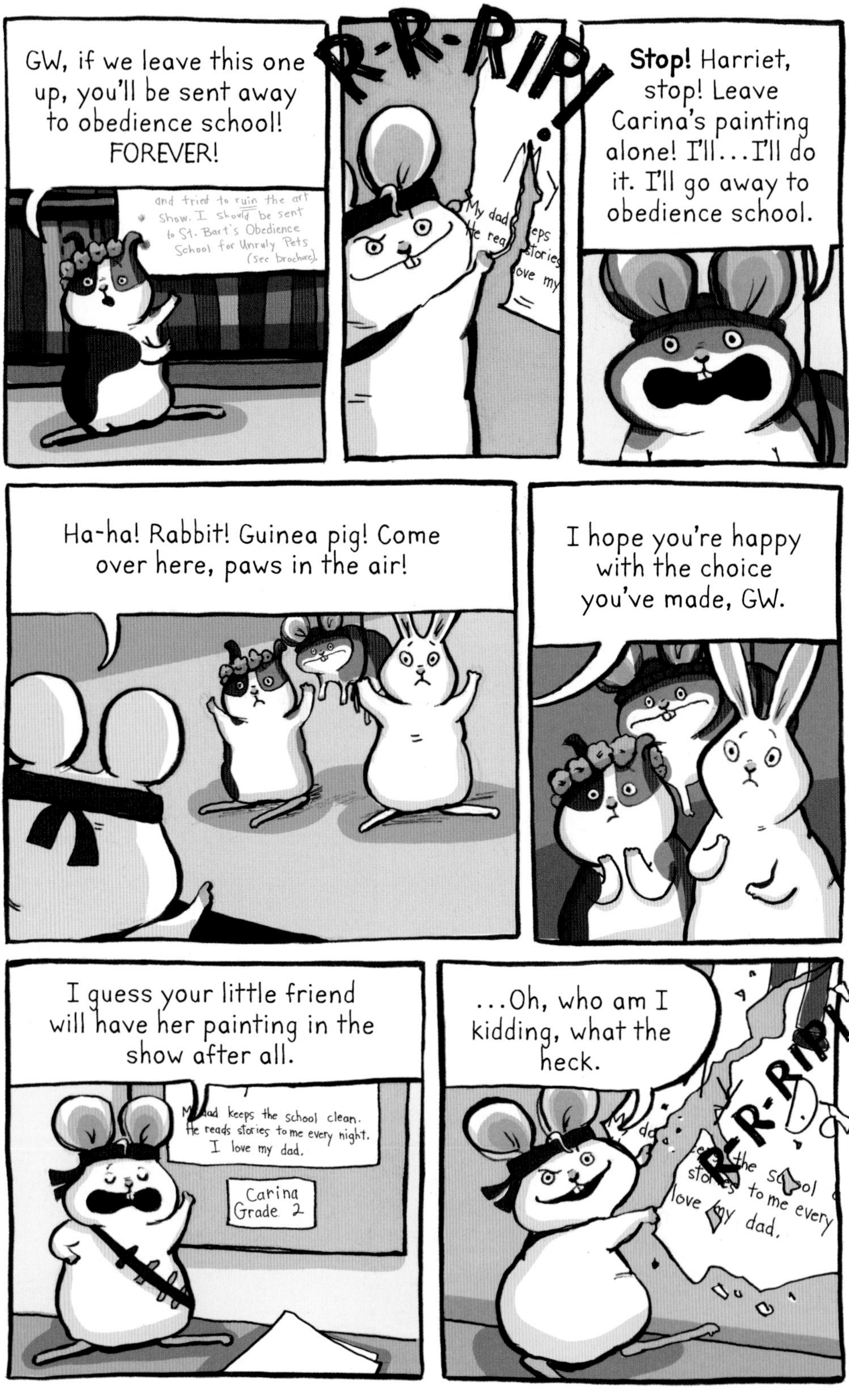
GW, if we leave this one up, you'll be sent away to obedience school! FOREVER!
and tried to ruin the art show. I should be sent to St. Bart's Obedience School for Unruly Pets (see brochure).
R-R-RIP!
Stop! Harriet, stop! Leave Carina's painting alone! I'll...I'll do it. I'll go away to obedience school.
Ha-ha! Rabbit! Guinea pig! Come over here, paws in the air!
I hope you're happy with the choice you've made, GW.
I guess your little friend will have her painting in the show after all.
My dad keeps the school clean. He reads stories to me every night. I love my dad.
Carina Grade 2
...Oh, who am I kidding, what the heck.
R-R-RIP!

# Chapter 10

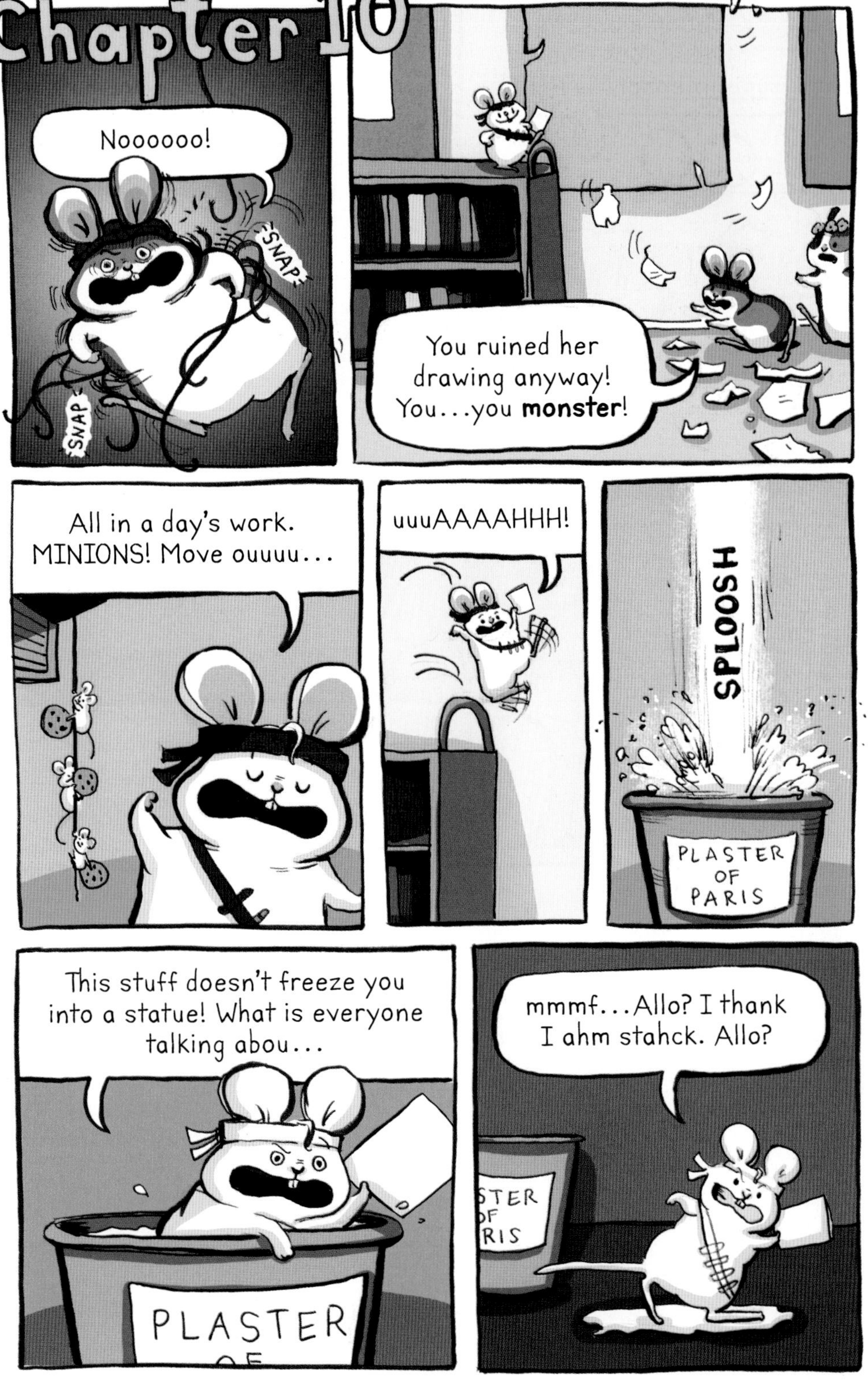

Nooooo!
SNAP
SNAP
You ruined her drawing anyway! You...you **monster**!
All in a day's work. MINIONS! Move ouuuu...
uuuAAAAHHH!
SPLOOSH
PLASTER OF PARIS
This stuff doesn't freeze you into a statue! What is everyone talking abou...
PLASTER
mmmf...Allo? I thank I ahm stahck. Allo?

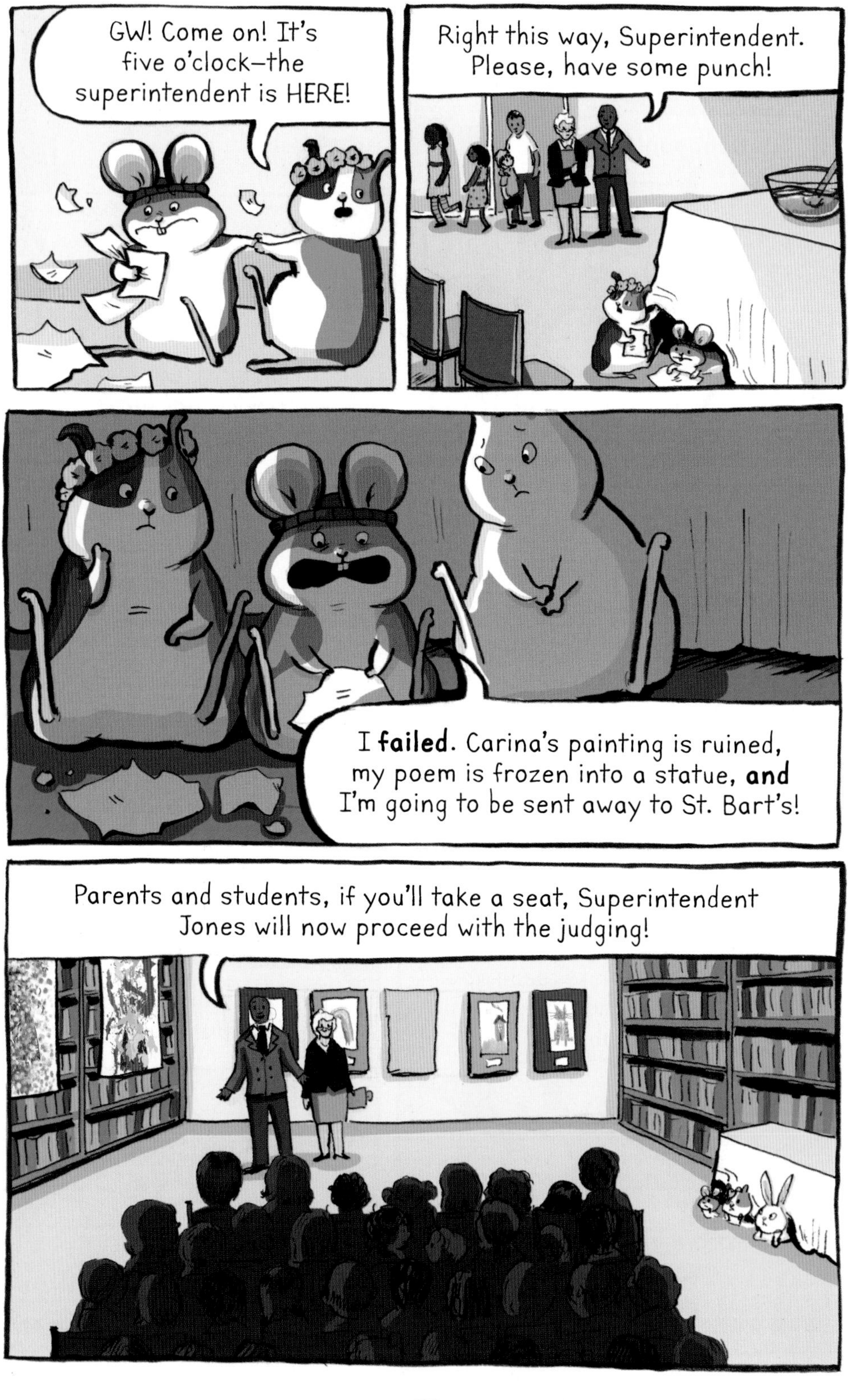
GW! Come on! It's five o'clock—the superintendent is HERE!
Right this way, Superintendent. Please, have some punch!
I **failed**. Carina's painting is ruined, my poem is frozen into a statue, **and** I'm going to be sent away to St. Bart's!
Parents and students, if you'll take a seat, Superintendent Jones will now proceed with the judging!

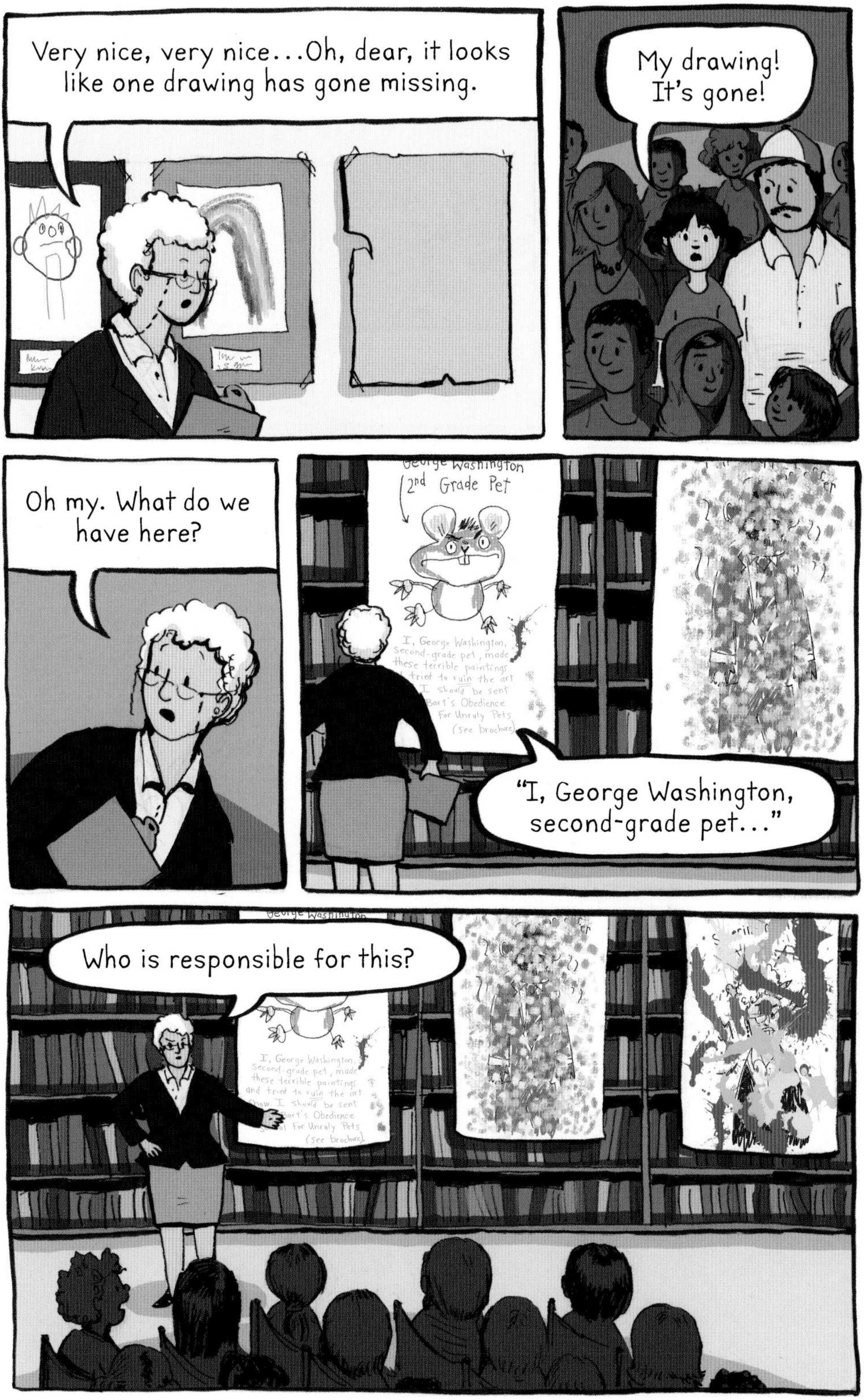

Very nice, very nice...Oh, dear, it looks like one drawing has gone missing.
My drawing! It's gone!
Oh my. What do we have here?
"I, George Washington, second-grade pet..."
Who is responsible for this?

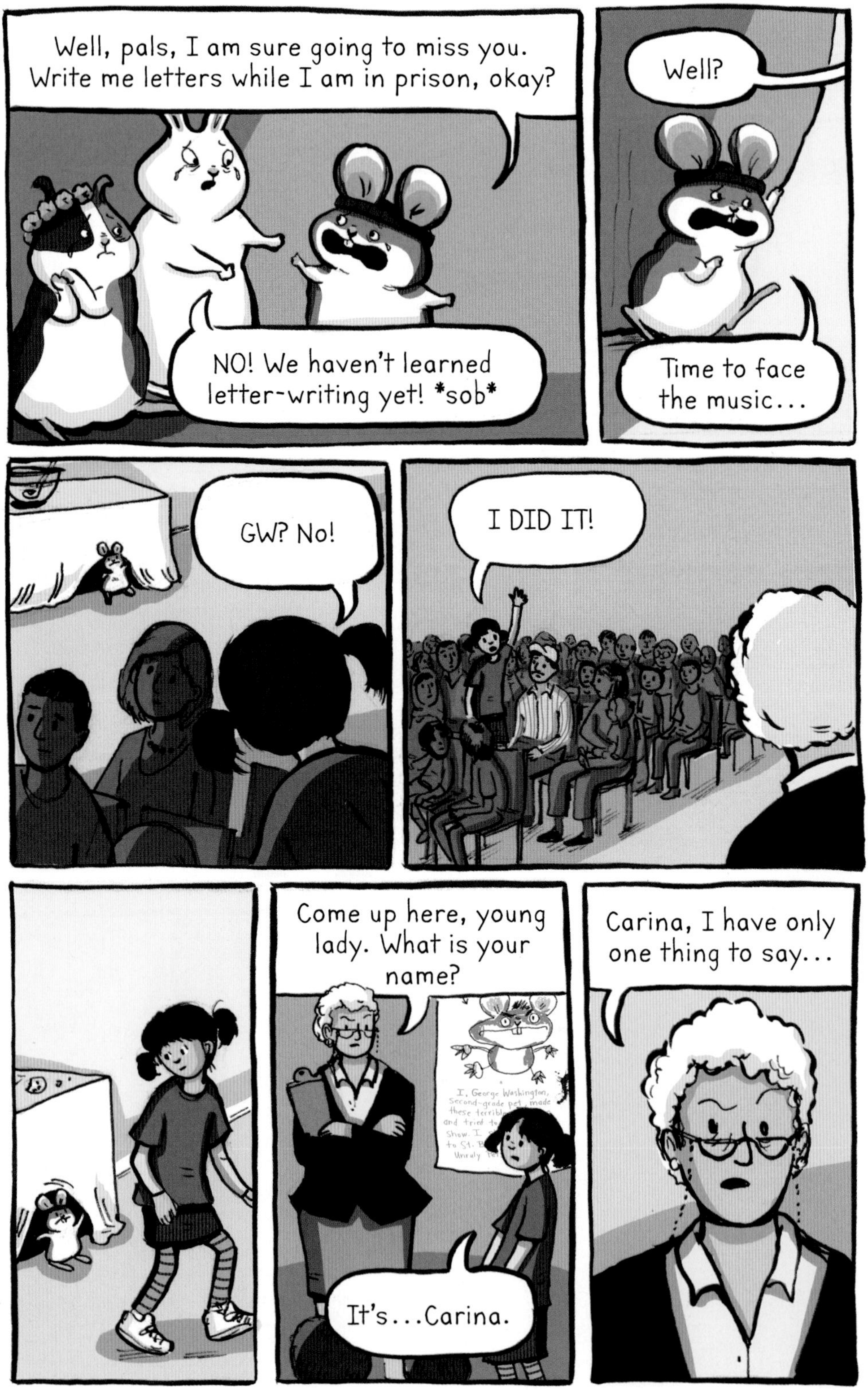
Well, pals, I am sure going to miss you. Write me letters while I am in prison, okay?
NO! We haven't learned letter-writing yet! *sob*
Well?
Time to face the music...
GW? No!
I DID IT!
Come up here, young lady. What is your name?
It's...Carina.
Carina, I have only one thing to say...

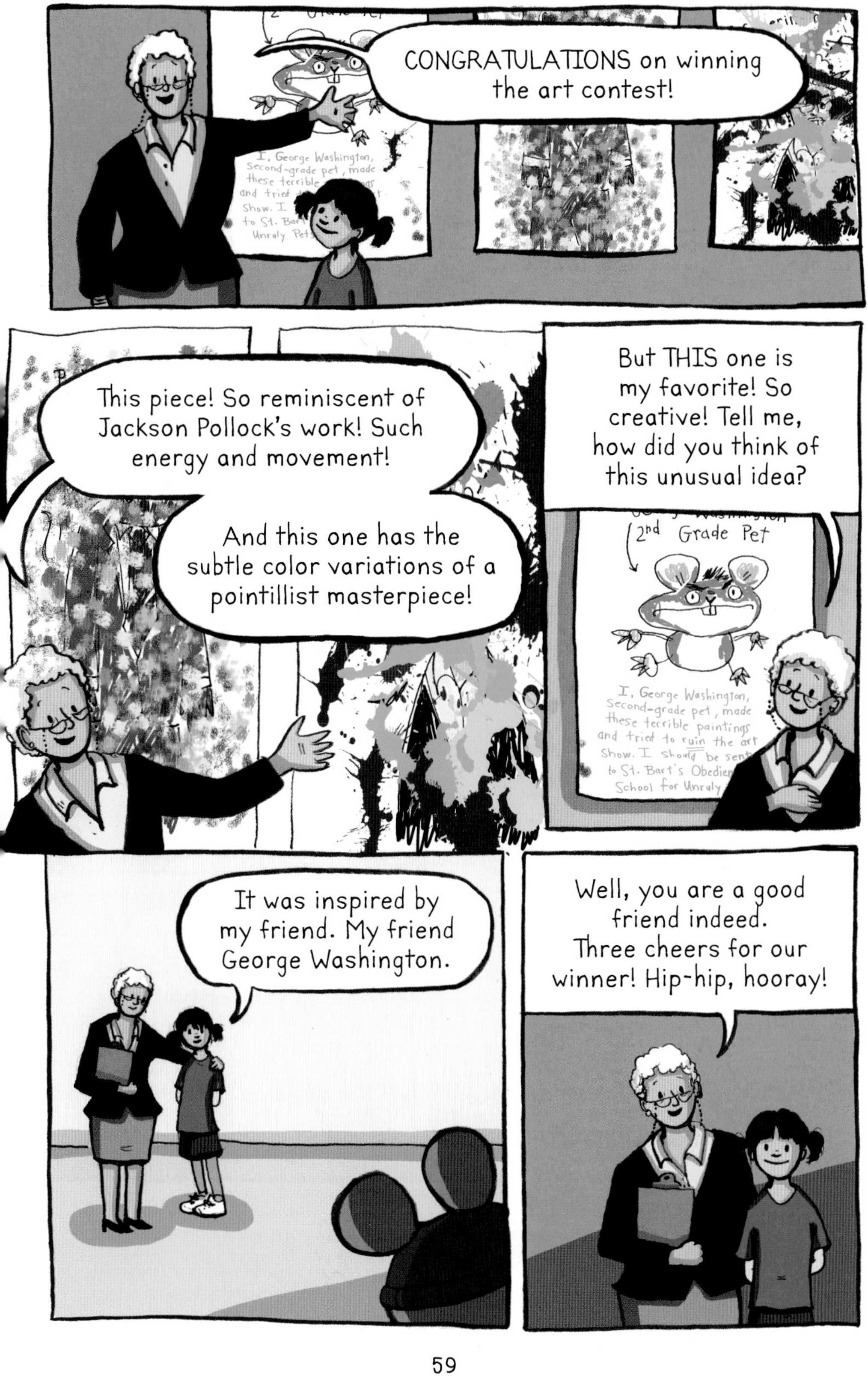
CONGRATULATIONS on winning the art contest!
This piece! So reminiscent of Jackson Pollock's work! Such energy and movement!
And this one has the subtle color variations of a pointillist masterpiece!
But THIS one is my favorite! So creative! Tell me, how did you think of this unusual idea?
2nd Grade Pet
I, George Washington, Second-grade pet, made these terrible paintings and tried to ruin the art Show. I should be sent to St. Bart's Obedien School for Unruly
It was inspired by my friend. My friend George Washington.
Well, you are a good friend indeed. Three cheers for our winner! Hip-hip, hooray!

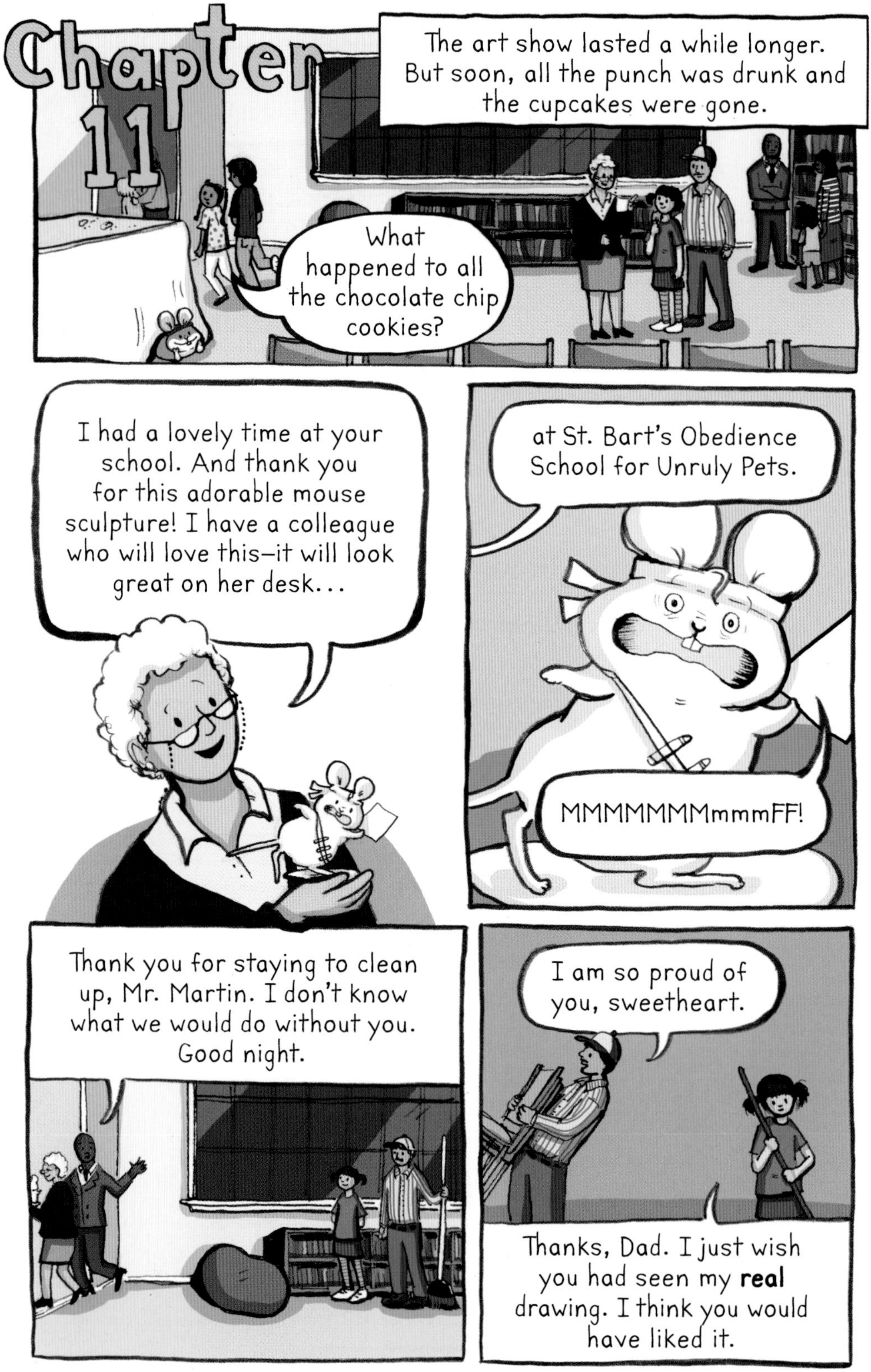
Chapter 11
The art show lasted a while longer. But soon, all the punch was drunk and the cupcakes were gone.
What happened to all the chocolate chip cookies?
I had a lovely time at your school. And thank you for this adorable mouse sculpture! I have a colleague who will love this—it will look great on her desk...
at St. Bart's Obedience School for Unruly Pets.
MMMMMMMmmmFF!
Thank you for staying to clean up, Mr. Martin. I don't know what we would do without you. Good night.
I am so proud of you, sweetheart.
Thanks, Dad. I just wish you had seen my **real** drawing. I think you would have liked it.

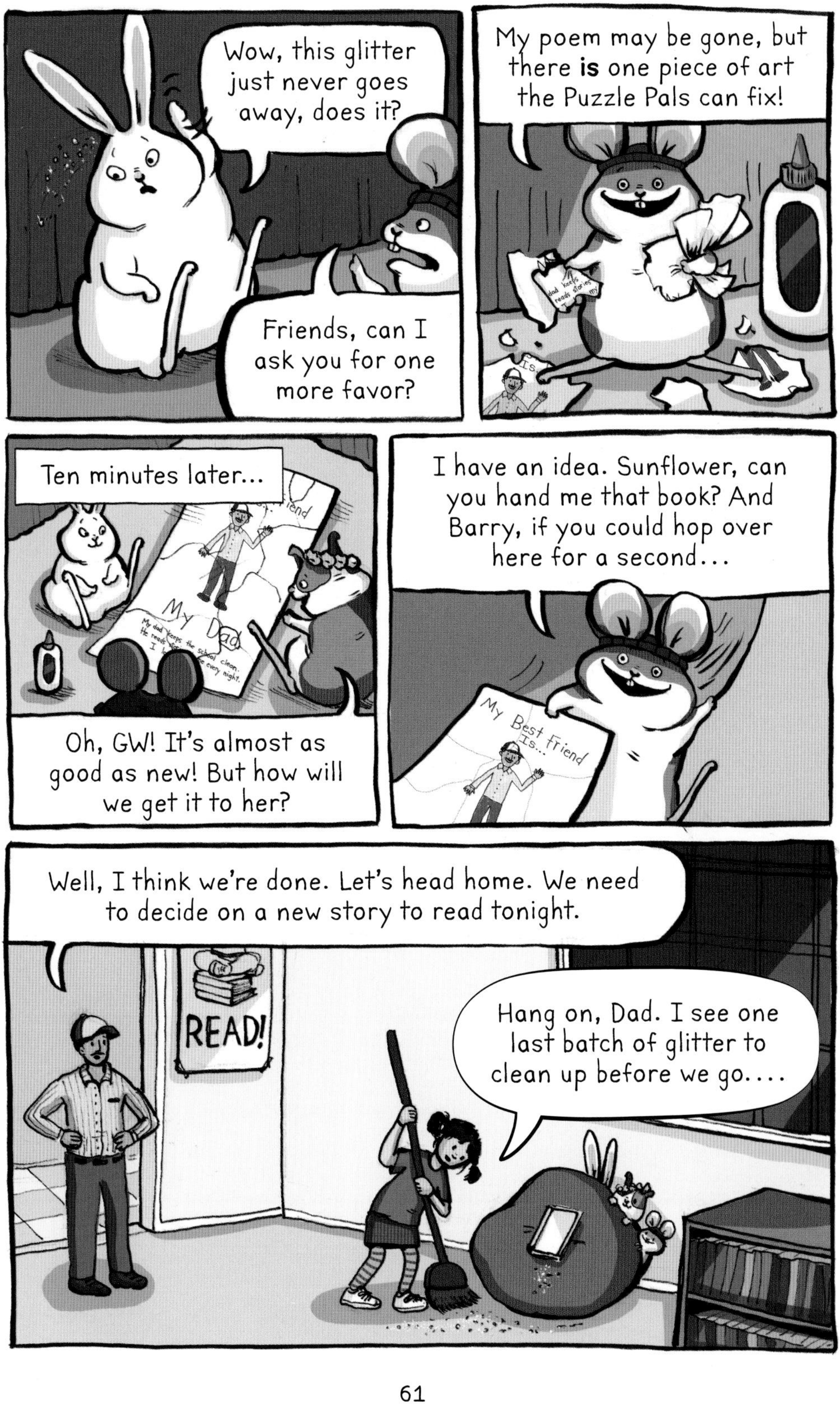
Wow, this glitter just never goes away, does it?
Friends, can I ask you for one more favor?
My poem may be gone, but there **is** one piece of art the Puzzle Pals can fix!
Ten minutes later...
My Dad
Oh, GW! It's almost as good as new! But how will we get it to her?
I have an idea. Sunflower, can you hand me that book? And Barry, if you could hop over here for a second...
My Best Friend Is...
Well, I think we're done. Let's head home. We need to decide on a new story to read tonight.
READ!
Hang on, Dad. I see one last batch of glitter to clean up before we go....

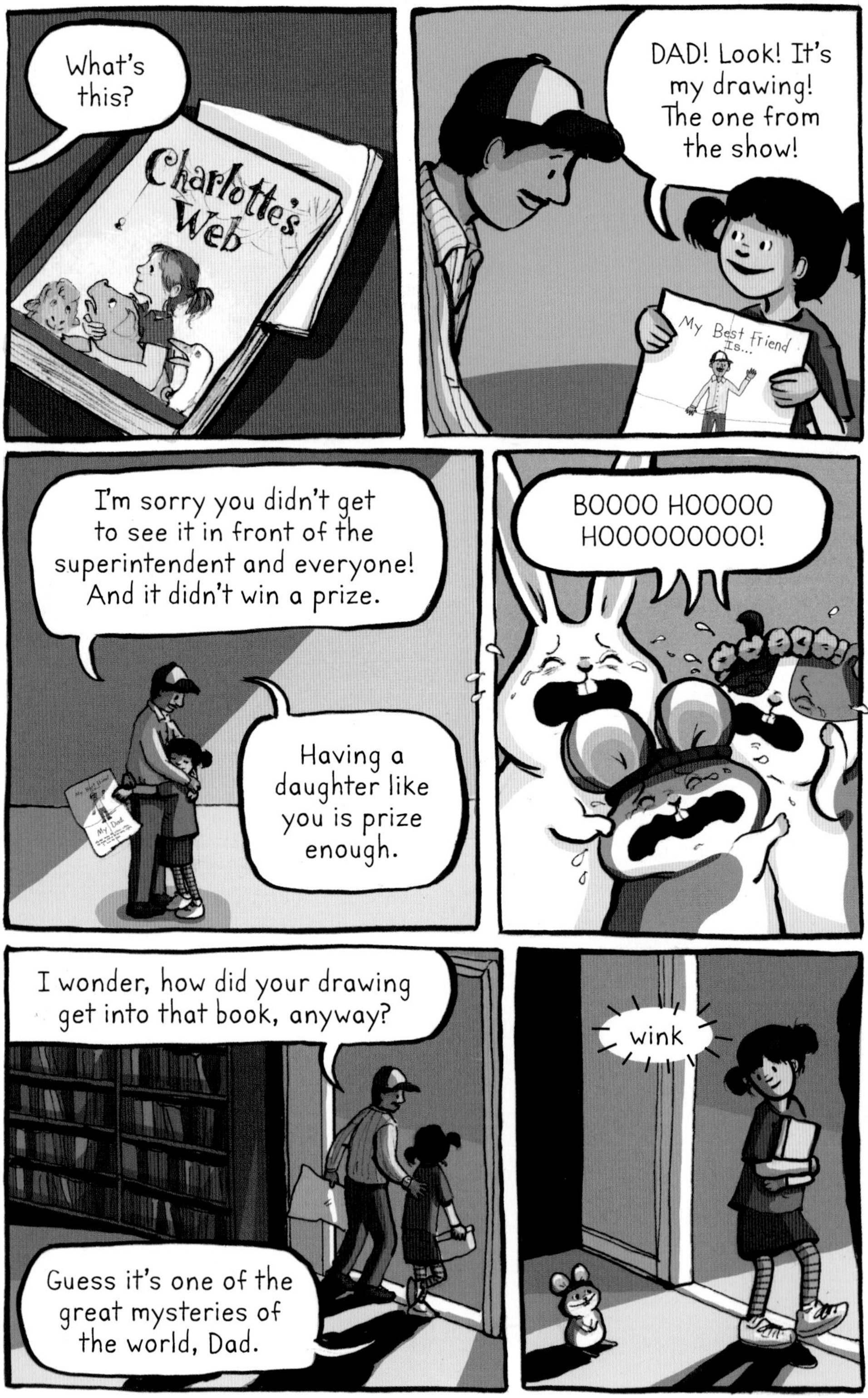
What's this?
Charlotte's Web
DAD! Look! It's my drawing! The one from the show!
My Best Friend Is...
I'm sorry you didn't get to see it in front of the superintendent and everyone! And it didn't win a prize.
Having a daughter like you is prize enough.
BOOOO HOOOOO HOOOOOOOOO!
I wonder, how did your drawing get into that book, anyway?
Guess it's one of the great mysteries of the world, Dad.
wink

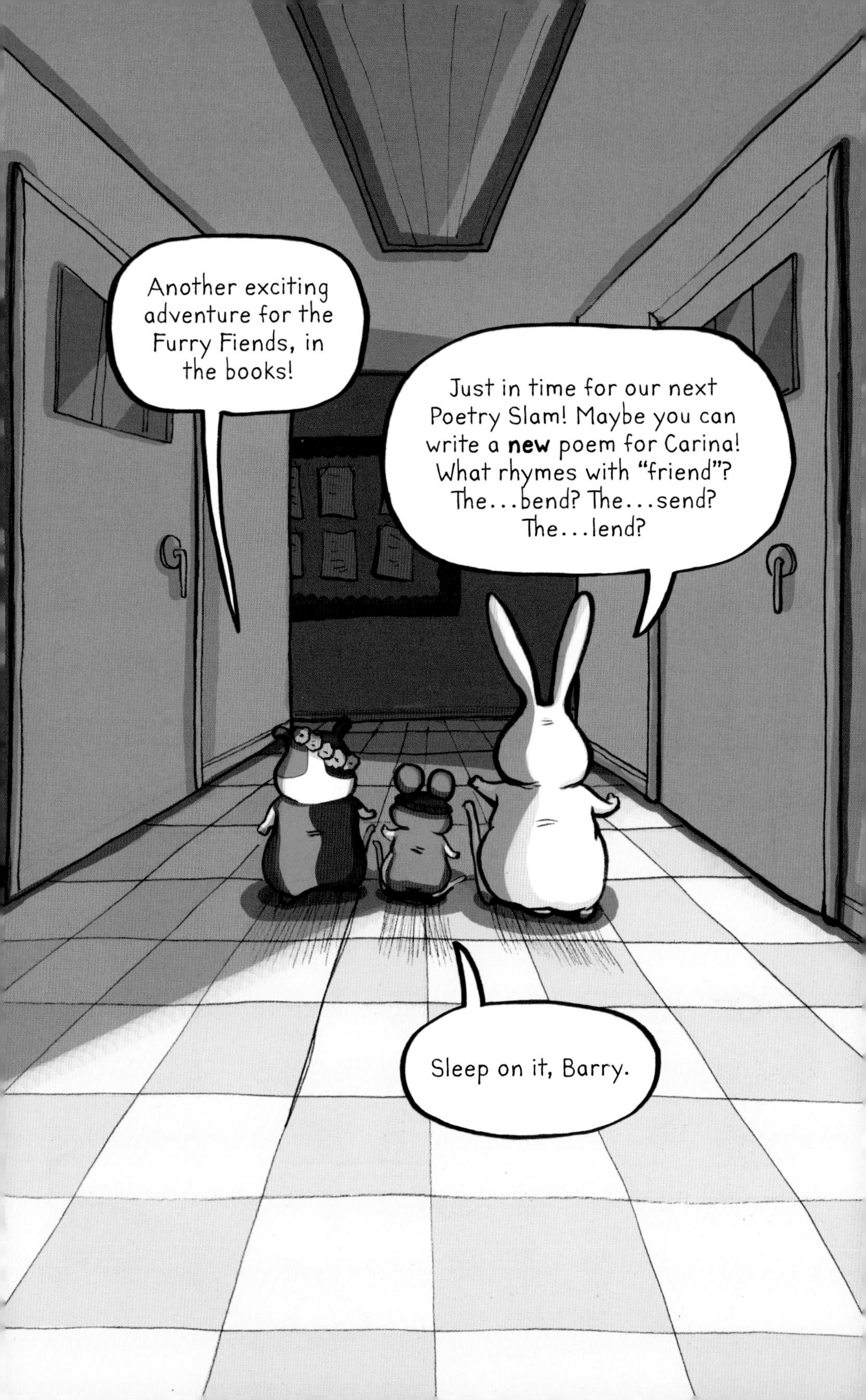
Another exciting adventure for the Furry Fiends, in the books!
Just in time for our next Poetry Slam! Maybe you can write a **new** poem for Carina! What rhymes with "friend"? The...bend? The...send? The...lend?
Sleep on it, Barry.

THE ~~TEND~~ ~~BEND~~ ~~SEND~~ . . . END.

To Mom and Dad, for the inspiration.

Henry Holt and Company
*Publishers since 1866*
175 Fifth Avenue
New York, New York 10010
mackids.com

Henry Holt® is a registered trademark of Macmillan Publishing Group, LLC.
Copyright © 2017 by Victoria Jamieson. All rights reserved.

Library of Congress Control Number: 2016949882

ISBN (HC) 978-1-62779-118-2
3 5 7 9 10 8 6 4

ISBN (PB) 978-1-62779-119-9
3 5 7 9 10 8 6 4 2

Our books may be purchased in bulk for promotional, educational, or business use.
Please contact your local bookseller or the Macmillan Corporate and Premium Sales Department
at (800) 221-7945 ext. 5442 or by e-mail at MacmillanSpecialMarkets@macmillan.com.

First Edition—2017
The artist used pen and ink with color added digitally to create the illustrations for this book.
Printed in China by Toppan Leefung Printing Ltd.,
Dongguan City, Guangdong Province

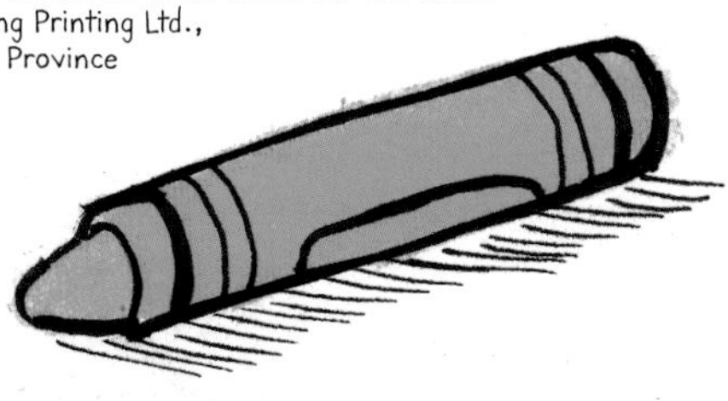